Charles Elmer Allison

A Historical Sketch of Hamilton College, Clinton, New York

Charles Elmer Allison

A Historical Sketch of Hamilton College, Clinton, New York

ISBN/EAN: 9783337416300

Printed in Europe, USA, Canada, Australia, Japan

Cover: Foto ©Andreas Hilbeck / pixelio.de

More available books at **www.hansebooks.com**

A

HISTORICAL SKETCH

OF

HAMILTON COLLEGE,

CLINTON, NEW YORK.

———

BY THE

REV. CHARLES ELMER ALLISON,

CLASS OF 1870.

YONKERS, NEW YORK,
1889.

PREFACE.

An article, written for the columns of a newspaper, was the nucleus of these pages. Several alumni desired to have the newspaper sketch in a form more convenient for preservation and reference. Without recasting the original sketch, additions were made, among them records previously published by the College. Although the author of this book, with more propriety, might have made an appendix of those records, they were incorporated in the present form. Graduates and other readers, conversant with the annals of the College, will justly regard this volume a compilation rather than a well-digested history. At best, it is only a sketch. Folios would not suffice to record the labors and achievements of eminent alumni, whose names even, do not appear on these pages. For example, only a brief mention is made of missionary graduates,—" God's Chivalry."

When Samuel Kirkland, himself a missionary, made his weary way into the forest gloom, and subsequently founded in the woods an institution of Christian learning, little did he realize that many, who should tread those walks beneath the poplar trees on College Hill, would afterward, with feet beautiful upon the mountains of distant lands, bring to dying souls, with tongue, pen and press, the same good tidings, and publish the same peace he proclaimed to his dusky disciples. As for those faithful missionaries, they neither seek nor need earthly honor. Are not their names and achievements written in the chronicles of the King, whose they are and whom they serve? There they will shine.

3

PREFACE.

"When the stars are old, and the sun is cold,
And the leaves of the judgment book unfold."

Imperfect as this little volume is, it serves to unbosom its author's love for his ALMA MATER—an Institution associated in his mind and heart with student friends and loved instructors, with home and parents, whose lives were rich in counsel and sweet with tenderness, and but for whose self-sacrificing affection he could not have enjoyed the advantages of the College.

It is hoped that the book will enable widely-scattered graduates, (whose feet have wandered far since, with unexhausted energy, they trod the winding paths of the campus), to stand once more, surrounded by "the boys," in the shadows of the grey halls, from whose windows so many years ago, they eagerly looked out upon life with its untasted joys and unfinished work. Many of them are now "looking out of life's western windows." Possibly a loved name, or pictured college hall, or familiar face in this volume will cause the dimming eyes of some old graduate to "burn again under his white hair as fire burns on the hearth when there is snow on the roof."

"Knowledge is folly unless grace guide it," for the fear of the Lord is the beginning of wisdom. A college without Christ cannot permanently prosper, nor can it be loved as a Christian College is. Hamilton is conservative. True to her motto, *Lux et Veritas*, she advocates for the mind old-fashioned culture and for the priceless soul, "the faith which was once delivered to the saints." If these pages shall, even in a slight degree, promote the prosperity of our Mother on the Hill, the author will not regret that, for their preparation, he took up the pen which he now lays down.

C. E. A.

*Pastor's Study, Dayspring Presbyterian Church,
Yonkers, N. Y., April 15th, 1889.*

CORRIGENDA

Page 10. line 10. *for* Wesleyen *read* Wes'eyan.

Page 11. line 13. *for* Jay *read* Jas.

Page 18. line 31. *for* Chieftan *read* Chieftain.

Page 20. line 33. *for* 1793 *read* 1794.

Page 21. line 7. *for* ninety-three *read* ninety-two.

Page 23. lines 19, 20, 21 *should be omitted. They perpetuate an error which has crept into the College annals. Professor Norton was not the author of the hymn referred to.*

Page 24. line 39. *for* advioe *read* advice.

Page 26. line 15. *after* brine *insert* '

Page 29. line 2. *after* sorrow *insert* "

Page 40. line 6. *(beginning of line.) for* Kirkland *read* Edmund Wetmore.

Page 63, lines 13, 14, 19, 22 *for* " *insert* '

Page 64. lines 13, 16 *for* " *insert* '

Page 64. line 23. *after* Hamilton *insert* "

Page 66. lines 3, 4 *for* " *insert* '

Page 67. line 12. *for* adequate *read* inadequate.

Page 69. line 2. *for* Vermillion *read* Vermilion.

Page 76. line 17. *for* siderial *read* sidereal.

Page 77. line 22. *for* " " *insert* ' '"

Page 79. line 24. *for* 1793 *read* 1794.

Page 80. line 4. *for* indispensible *read* indispensable.

Page 81. line 17. *for* " " *insert* ' '

Page 81. line 24. *for* " " *insert* ' '

Index page I. *omit* 14 *after* Amherst College.

Index-page V. *under* Hymns *insert* "Welcome thou servant of the Lord." 59. *omit*, "Ye servants of God your Master proclaim." 23.

Index-page VI. *for* Wm. W. 62. *read* Wm. N. 62.

Index-page VIII. line 9. *for* 5 *read* 6.

Index-page IX. *for* Wesleyen *read* Wesleyan.

HAMILTON ONEIDA ACADEMY,

FOUNDED BY SAMUEL KIRKLAND IN 1793.

———

HAMILTON COLLEGE,

CHARTERED IN 1812.

———

"No great history of our government can be written which does not make this state of New York its central point. As this truth shall be impressed upon our people, not only will the interest in the character of SAMUEL KIRKLAND increase, but the College he founded as a means of education to the Indian, as well as the white man, will be regarded as a memorial of a race which at one time held despotic rule over a region greatly exceeding the united territories of France and Britain. The relationship of its Founder to the long line of missionaries, who for a century labored with savage tribes in danger and suffering, will give to the College a sacredness in its religious aspect. It will not be merely a memorial of the past, for it fittingly crowns the range of hills from which flow the rivers that bind together our union with silver bands. It overlooks valleys once travelled by armies in war, which are the channels of commerce in peace, and which will be in the future what they have been in the past, the pathways of great events."

HORATIO SEYMOUR.

"We would have no compromise with infidelity or skepticism ; we are Christian educators ; we prize God's word above all earthly science. There is our banner : We fling it to the breeze ! If you send your son hither ; we shall do all that in us lies to teach him what this book contains, and to make its truths effective in the control of his life. We shall not apologize for Christianity, nor treat it as a hand-maid to natural science : but as the queen-regent over all our studies ; our richest possession in time, our only hope for eternity."

PRESIDENT FISHER.

HISTORICAL SKETCH OF

HAMILTON COLLEGE.

CLINTON, Oneida Co., N. Y., is widely known, not only as the seat of Hamilton College, but as a village of Grammar schools and ladies' seminaries. It is near the center of the Empire State. The beautiful college town nestles in a tranquil valley,

> " Where the Oriskany winding flows,
> And tells its story as it goes,
> Of warrior bold and Indian maid."

The nearest city, (Utica,) is nine miles away, twenty-five minutes by rail. Clintonians are justly proud of their academic village. Recently with much pomp and display they commemorated the one hundredth anniversary of the settlement of the place. The President of the United States was present. President Cleveland, when a youth, studied in the Clinton Grammar School, preparing to enter Hamilton College, but the death of his father, a Presbyterian minister, frustrated his hopes. His brother, also a minister of the gospel, graduated at the College, and his cultured sister, Rose E. Cleveland, graduated at Houghton, one of the Clinton seminaries for young ladies.

Years ago students reached Clinton by stages, the more fortunate securing seats within the lumbering vehicles, and teaching some fair fellow-traveller how to conjugate *Amo*, while the less fortunate, perched themselves on the outside, and sang their student-songs—" Litoria," or " I sat upon the quarter deck, and whiffed my cares away," or " Its the way we have at old Hamilton," or,

> *" Gaudeamus igitur*
> *" Juvenes dum sumus,*
> *" Post jucundam juventutem*
> *" Post molestam senectutem*
> *" Nos habebit humus."*

College Hill in Clinton commands a magnificent view. It is reached by College Street, the longest avenue in the beautiful town. Between the foot of the hill and the College campus, the street is divided into four parts, known far and wide, among all Hamilton men, as Freshman hill, Sophomore hill, Junior hill and Senior hill. For nearly a century students have been treading that famous hillside walk. So many have left those winding paths to render Church and State large service and, as alumni, to climb to undying fame, that when the long procession moves before the eye of the scribe up the historic slope, under the sentinel poplars, through the grey halls, and out into the world, he does not wonder that successive graduating classes, about to say farewell to the College, salute the weather-beaten stone buildings with cheers and music.

> " For the good and the great, in their beautiful prime,
> Through these precincts have musingly trod,
> While they girded their spirits and deepened the streams,
> That make glad the fair City of God."

If those who compile the Triennial Catalogues of Hamilton, would publish, as some other colleges do, the names of all students, whether graduates or not, the reader might know how many have studied within the walls of the old institution. Probably the number would approximate four thousand. Many who did not graduate have become eminent men and recall with pleasure and gratitude their student days at the College. The institution has been enriched by their gifts and rejoices in the laurels they have won. The whole number of graduates is over twenty-six hundred.

CLASSIFICATION OF THE ALUMNI

OF

HAMILTON COLLEGE, CLINTON, N. Y.

WHOLE NUMBER OF ALUMNI,	2605
STELLIGERENTS,	651
WHOLE NUMBER OF ALUMNI LIVING,	1954
GRADUATES OF THE MAYNARD LAW SCHOOL,	261
LAWYERS,	485
CLERGYMEN,	713
CLERGYMEN IN THE SYNOD OF NEW YORK,	143
FOREIGN MISSIONARIES,	34
MODERATORS OF THE PRESBYTERIAN GENERAL ASSEMBLY,	5
COMMISSIONERS TO THE GENERAL ASSEMBLY OF 1888,	13
MEMBERS OF CONGRESS,	29
STATE GOVERNORS,	5
STATE SENATORS,	26
MEMBERS OF STATE CONSTITUTIONAL CONVENTIONS,	13
SUPREME COURT JUDGES,	28
PRESIDENTIAL ELECTORS,	5
COLLEGE PRESIDENTS,	13
REGENTS OF THE UNIVERSITY OF THE STATE OF NEW YORK,	8
COLLEGE PROFESSORS AND TUTORS,	94
THEOLOGICAL SEMINARY PROFESSORS,	19
STATE SUPERINTENDENTS OF PUBLIC INSTRUCTION,	6
NORMAL SCHOOL PRINCIPALS AND PROFESSORS,	16
PRINCIPALS OF ACADEMIES AND HIGH SCHOOLS,	119
PHYSICIANS,	88
BANKERS AND BROKERS,	49
EDITORS,	82
AGRICULTURISTS,	24
MERCHANTS,	49
CIVIL ENGINEERS AND ARCHITECTS,	15
MANUFACTURERS,	20
ENLISTED IN THE WAR FOR THE UNION,	174

BRIEF ROLL OF EMINENT HAMILTONIANS.

The roll of graduates carries the names of the Rev. Dr. Edward
Robinson, Ex. U. S. Senator David Jewitt Baker, Hon. Charles P.
Kirkland, Hon. Gerrit Smith, the Rev. Dr. Stephen W. Taylor.
first President of Madison University, Hamilton, N. Y., the Rev
Albert Barnes, Prof. Charles Avery, Judge W. J. Bacon of the
Supreme Court, Dr. Samuel B. Woolworth, Secretary of the Board
of University Regents, Vice-Chancellor Geo. W. Clinton, the Rev.
Dr. Asa Mahan, Ex-President of Oberlin College, the Rev. Dr.
Augustus W. Smith, Ex-President of Wesleyen University, the
Rev. Dr. Daniel D. Whedon, Dr. A. C. Kendrick, Professor of
Greek in Rochester University, and Member of the American
Committee for the Revision of the New Testament, United States
Senator Henry B. Payne, Hon. A. P. Willard, Ex-Gov. of Indiana,
Dr. John N. Pomeroy, the well known jurist and legal author,
whose portrait the University of New York has just hung on her
walls, and to whose memory the University of California has
erected a statue, Dr. William Hague, Dr. Oren Root, Dr. Theo.
W. Dwight, of the Columbia College Law School, Dr. Edward
North, the Rev. Dr. Anson J. Upson, Professor in Auburn Theol.
Seminary, the Rev. Dr. James Eells, Professor in Theol. Seminary,
San Francisco, and in Lane Theol. Seminary, the Rev. Dr. Thos.
S. Hastings, President of Union Theol. Seminary, N. Y. City, Ex.
U. S. Senator Daniel D. Pratt, U. S. Senator Joseph R. Hawley,
Dr. Edward Orton, Ex. Pres. of Antioch College and of Ohio State
University, and State Geologist, the Rev. Dr. Joel Parker, the
Rev. Dr. Alex. McLean, Sec. American Bible Society, the Rev.
Dr. Frank F. Ellinwood, Sec. Presbyterian Board of Foreign
Missions, the Rev. Dr. Henry Kendall, Secretary Presbyterian
Board of Home Missions, the Rev. Dr. Herrick Johnson of the
Presbyterian Board of Aid for Colleges, the Rev. Dr. Henry A.
Nelson, Editor of " The Church at Home and Abroad," the official
organ of the Presbyterian Church in the United States, the Rev.
Dr. Arthur T. Pierson, Joint-Editor of the " The Missionary
Review," the Rt. Rev. Dr. Theo. B. Lyman, Bishop of North Caro-
lina, the Rev. Dr. Wm. E. Knox, Dr. D. H. Cochran, President of
Brooklyn Polytechnic, Dr. Isaac H. Hall, the scholar and anti-
quarian, Dr. Edwin C. Litchfield, who endowed the Litchfield
Observatory, Hamilton College, Dr. John A. Paine, Dr. W. C.

1. THE REV. ALBERT BARNES, '25.
3. THE REV. DR. HENRY A. NELSON, '41.
5. THE REV. DR. THOS S. HASTINGS, '48.
7. THE REV. DR. HERRICK JOHNSON, '57.

2. THE REV. DR. JOEL PARKER, '24.
4. THE REV. DR. HENRY KENDALL, '41.
6. THE REV. DR. FRANK F. ELLINWOOD, '53.
8. THE REV. DR. ARTHUR T. PIERSON, '56.

Winslow, the Egyptologist. Hon. G. W. Scofield, Judge of the Court of Claims at Washington, and President of the Washington Hamilton Alumni Association, Brigadier General John Cochrane, Charles Dudley Warner, Hon. John Jay Knox, Ex-Comptroller of the United States Currency, Hon. Abram B. Weaver, Hon. Chau Laisun, Chinese Commissioner of Education, Professors D. W. Fiske, S. G. Williams, Francis M. Burdick, Geo. Prentice Bristol, Brainard G. Smith, (Chair of Journalism,) and Dr. A. C. White of the Cornell University Faculty, Dr. Henry A. Frink of the Amherst College Faculty, Prof. Chas. A. Borst of Johns Hopkins University, Prof. Jermain G. Porter, Director of Observatory at Cincinnati, Ohio, Professors Kelsey, Hopkins, Root, Brandt, Hoyt, Evans, and Scollard of the Hamilton College Faculty, the late John Jay Lewis of the Madison University Faculty, the Rev. Dr. Charles E. Knox, President of the German Theol. Seminary, Newark, New Jersey, the Rev. Dr. Willis J. Beecher, Professor of Hebrew in Auburn Theol. Seminary, Professor Charles K. Hoyt of Wells College, Dr. Adelbert J. Schlager, Professor of Hebrew in the German Theol. Seminary, Dubuque, Iowa, the Rev Dr. Wm. A. Bartlett, Washington D. C., Hon. Elihu Root, Ex-United States Attorney, New York City, Hon. R. A. Elmer, Ex-Second Assistant Postmaster-General, Judge Charles H. Truax, Ex-Pres. N. Y. Association of Hamilton Alumni, Judge Alfred C. Coxe, the Rev. Dr. J. H. Ecob of Albany, the Rev. Dr. Rufus S. Green, President of the Buffalo Hamilton College Alumni Association, the Rev. Dr. David R. Breed, President of Western Association of Hamilton Alumni, the Rev. M. Woolsey Stryker, and the Rev. Charles F. Goss of the Chicago pulpit, the Rev. Dr. George William Knox, Professor in Imperial University, Tokyo, Japan, the Rev. Dr. Edward C. Ray of Topeka, Kansas, the Rev. Dr. Wm. N. Page, Ex-President of the Mid-Continent Association of Hamilton Alumni, the Rev. Dr. Robert L. Bachman of Utica, A. H. Eaton, M. D., Prof. Henry B. Millard, M. D., Seldon H. Talcott, M. D., Chief of Corps of Physicians, Middletown State Asylum, A. Norton Brockway, M. D., Trustee of Hamilton College, Emmons Clark, Col. of 7th Reg., N. Y. City, Hon. Horatio C. Burchard, Ex-Superintendent of U. S. Mint at Philadelphia, Hon Wm. J. Wallace, LL. D., Judge U. S. Circuit Court, N. Y. State, Judge Joseph S. Bosworth, Metropolitan Police Commissioner, N. Y. City, Hon. Milton H. Merwin, Judge of New York State Supreme Court,

Hon. William H. H. Miller, United States Attorney-General, Hon. Willard A. Cobb, Regent of the University and editor of the Lockport *Daily Journal*, Milton H. Northrup, of the Syracuse *Courier*, S. N. D. North, formerly of the Albany *Express*, now editor of the *Quarterly Bulletin* of the National Association of Wool Growers, Chester S. Lord, managing editor of the New York *Sun*, E. M. Rewey, also of the New York *Sun*, A. L. Blair, of the Troy *Daily Times*, Henry C. Maine, of the Rochester *Democrat and Chronicle*, George E. Durham, editor-in-chief of the Utica *Press*, and Hon. Fred. Dick, State Superintendent of Public Schools, Colorado. Many other honored names are recorded in the Catalogue of Hamilton graduates.

The College also has a long roll of honor, luminous with the names of patriot scholars, "History's graduates." The wealthy American, who will erect on College Hill a monument to the memory of these heroes, who laid down their pens to grasp swords and do battle for native land, will honor himself while honoring them. Hamilton furnished to the army 110 officers, 14 Chaplains, 9 Surgeons, and 41 private soldiers—174 in all.

The scholarship and services of the College have been recognized by other learned bodies. One turning the pages of the *Catalogus Collegii Hamiltonensis* reads the names of many colleges which have titled Hamilton Alumni. Among them the University of Halle, Germany, Harvard, Yale, Columbia, Princeton, Amherst, Brown, Rutgers, Union, Madison, Lafayette, Marietta, New York University, Wabash, University of Vermont, Dartmouth, Bowdoin, University of Wooster, Williams and Knox. With pardonable pride the Editor of the Alumniana in the Hamilton Literary Monthly writes at the head of his department, " *Quae regio in terris nostri non plena laboris?* "

An institution of learning which has graduated so many eminent men and in which, to-day, New England, the Middle, Southern, and Western States and foreign countries are represented by under-graduates, commands attention. Its history must interest all who are of a studious habit. An American scholar, who had been listening to the chronicles of Hamilton College said, "Surely the history of an institution of learning is a source of a part of its influence upon the students." For this reason many prefer " a college with the ivy on it." The vine of history creeps over the old college at Clinton.

HON. WM. H. H. MILLER,
CLASS OF 1861.,
ATTORNEY-GENERAL OF THE UNITED STATES.

THE ROMANS OF AMERICA.

Long before the settlement of the Mohawk valley by the whites, French and English statesmen and churchmen were turning their attention to central and western New York—a region inhabited by the Six Nations, "The Romans of America," who were savages, fierce, wild and cruel, but were also a heroic and patriotic people. They were brave and skilful warriors, wise legislators, keen diplomatists and eloquent orators. In all these respects they towered above all other tribes on this continent. In regard to their oratory, the historian SMITH states that in his day, "The art of public speaking is in high esteem among the Indians and much studied." They are extremely fond of method, and are displeased with any irregular harangue, because it is difficult to be remembered. Benjamin Franklin wrote a brief paper about the Indians of North America. He said, "The Indian men, when young, are hunters and warriors; when old, counselors; for all their government is by the counsel or advice of the sages, there is no force, there are no prisons, no officers to compel obedience, or inflict punishment. Hence they generally study oratory, the best speaker having the most influence. The Indian women till the ground, dress the food, nurse and bring up the children, and preserve and hand down to posterity the memory of public transactions. These employments of men and women are accounted natural and honorable. Having few artificial wants, they have abundance of leisure for improvement in conversation. Having frequent occasions to hold public councils, they have acquired great order and decency in conducting them. The old men sit in the foremost ranks, the warriors in the next, and the women and children in the hindmost. The business of the women is to take exact notice of what passes, imprint it on their memories—for they have no writing—and communicate it to the children. They are the records of the council, and they preserve tradition of the stipulations in treaties a hundred years back; which, when we compare with our writings, we always find exact. He that would speak rises. The rest observe a profound silence. When he has finished and sits down, they leave him five or six minutes to recollect, that if he has omitted anything he intended to say, or has any thing to add, he may rise and deliver it. To interrupt another, even in common conversation, is reckoned highly indecent. How different is this from the conduct of a polite British House of Commons, where scarce a day passes without some confusion, that makes the speaker hoarse in calling *to order;* and how different from the mode of conversation in many polite companies of Europe, where, if you do not deliver your sentence with great rapidity, you are cut off in the middle of it by the impatient loquacity of those you converse with, and never suffered to finish it."

The Six Nations held in subjection a vast extent of country, and, in proportion to their numbers, they conquered more enemies and held more territory by force of arms than any people of which history gives an account, since the days of Alexander the Great. The Government which should secure the alliance, and the Church which should win the allegiance of these powerful tribes, might thereby hold supremacy on this continent. Should the New World, with its red men and its white settlers, be under the control of France or England? Statesmen in European council-chambers and warriors with swords and bayonets in American forests, and on American lakes, were answering that question. Zeal of Romanist and devotion of Protestant were aroused.

MISSIONARY ACTIVITY.

As early as 1641 flickering camp-fires in the Mohawk valley lighted up the faces of Jesuit missionaries. In 1700 all Jesuits were expelled by law from the State of New York. Protestant missionaries visited the Indian tribes in Central New York between 1712 and 1764. David Zeisberger and the Moravian Bishops visited Onondaga, and the tribe adopted him, but the French war thwarted the plans of this messenger of the Prince of Peace. Subsequently New England Christians brought Indians out of the forests and placed them in schools in Lebanon, Conn., and Stockbridge, Mass. A large number were at the latter school. At one time Jonathan Edwards had charge of their education. An Indian agent dealt so unjustly with some of the Indian students that they returned to their homes. Dr. Edwards lashed with stinging sentences the unsavory name of that agent. A Hamilton Alumnus has added, by way of a snapper to Dr. Edwards' lash, these lines. "Edwards' portraiture of this man is a master-piece. No jar of spirits ever preserved a reptile in more hideous life-likeness, no drop of amber ever revealed the head and

SAMUEL KIRKLAND

legs of a venomous insect more clearly than this man is embalmed in this monograph of the great theologian. It is significant that it was in the midst of his struggles with this poor miscreant that Edwards wrote his treatise on original sin."

SAMUEL KIRKLAND.

Among the students in Lebanon, Conn., was Samuel Kirkland. In him the historian is especially interested, because he became the missionary-founder of an institution of learning which was afterward chartered as Hamilton College. Kirkland came of good stock. Miles Standish was one of his progenitors. He was born in **1741**, and received his preparatory education at Dr. Wheel ock's Indian School in Lebanon. Dartmouth College grew out of that institution. The idea of the school had been suggested to Dr. Wheelock by his success in educating a young Mohican Indian, Samson Occum, who became a remarkable preacher, and who was the author of the hymn, "Awaked by Sinai's awful sound." The school was so much resorted to by native tribes that Dr. Wheelock determined to transfer it to some place nearer them. Hanover, New Hampshire, was selected, and when the institution was removed to that place it was chartered as Dartmouth College.

The late President Fisher, in a memorial address at a Hamilton College commencement, said: "It is well to notice that two of the leading colleges of this Union sprang from the spontaneous efforts of Missionaries, having primary references to the elevation of the Indian. Dartmouth and Hamilton are the outgrowth of Christianity in its purpose to rescue from degradation and lift up to a position of intelligence and true religion the Sons of the Forest. The tide of civilization, sweeping around and beyond them, has borne on its crest the wrecks and fragments of a once mighty nation. The providence of God, with other purposes in view, is working out through them, results broader and grander than even the seer-visioned men, who laid their foundations, foresaw. But while these Institutions live, they will lift up before the oncoming generations, in characters more durable than those chiseled in marble or brass, the fiery signal of the red denizens of the forest. And when thousands of names, once on the lips of millions, touched by the waters of Lethe, have sunk into oblivion, those of Wheelock and Kirkland the humble teachers of this race, will shine lustrous among the stars that gem the firmament of God."

From Lebanon young Kirkland went to Princeton College. Although not remaining to graduate with his class, he received his degree in course. While yet a college student, his heart burned within him as he thought of the untutored children of the woods. He knew that if he should go to them, many trials and hardships awaited him, "but none of these things moved him, neither counted he his life dear unto himself, so that he might finish his course with joy, and the ministry, which he had received of the Lord Jesus to testify the Gospel of the grace of God." Others had gone into the wilderness that the gloom there might be brightened with the healing beams of the Son of Righteousness. In 1765, the Princeton student, "a good man and full of the Holy Ghost," took his journey into the forest, leaving the world's honors for others to win. He went in the spirit of Him who said,

> "The vows
> Of God are on me, and I may not stop
> To play with shadows, or pluck earthly flowers
> Till I my work have done, and rendered up
> Account."

He accompanied two friendly Senecas to their tribe, which was the most westerly of the Six Nations. He knew that those nations were powerful, and in establishing missions among them he was following the examples of the early Apostles, who sought to preach the gospel in centers of influence. The Rev. Dr. Ellinwood, in an address delivered at Clinton, thus made reference to the devout ardor of the young scholar: "It was in January, 1765, that Samuel Kirkland, a student, not yet twenty-four years old, left Johnstown and plunged into the wilderness. On that cold winter morning, one hundred and twenty-four years ago, he had a dreary journey before him. With his two Indian guides he was to travel two hundred miles, his feet shod with snow-shoes, and on his back a pack of forty pounds, his path the trail in the snow made by the feet of his dusky leaders. He carried the germ and potency of Hamilton College. If the institution ever drifts from its Christian moorings, as some other colleges have, how unworthy will it be of its early history." No small part of the load which Kirkland and his guides carried in their knapsacks through the wilderness, consisted of choice treatises on Biblical learning.

His first work was among the Senecas. Subsequently he dwelt among the Oneidas, whom he esteemed the noblest of the Iroquois confederacy. Near the present village of Oneida Castle was an Indian village known as Kanonwarohale. There Kirkland lived for a time. To the log-house which he built with his own hands he brought his bride, a niece of President Wheelock, of Dartmouth. They journeyed by boat up the Mohawk river, and on horseback through the woods to Oneida, his wife on a pillion behind her husband. In this Indian village his two sons were born. The Indians gave them high-sounding names. One of them, John Thornton Kirkland, afterwards became distinguished as President of Harvard College.

During the Revolutionary war Kirkland was for a time a Chaplain in the American Army. It also fell to him to endeavor to keep the Six Nations in a state of neutrality. After the war he resumed his missionary labor. A Cayuga chief, who had heard favorable reports of "the white priest and his Bible," came sixty miles to visit him. In 1788 when George Clinton was Governor, the State of New York united with the Oneida Indians in making a grant of valuable land in Oneida County to the Rev. Samuel Kirkland, in recognition of his faithful services. The tract was two miles square. The eastern boundary of this plot was the "Property Line," which, at its intersection with College Street, Clinton, has been marked by a granite shaft, erected by the class of '87. The north-east corner of the tract was just outside the limits of the present beautiful campus.

"THE CRADLE OF HAMILTON COLLEGE."

In 1789 Kirkland cleared a few acres and built a log-house. A year or two later, probably in 1791, he built a small frame house, seventeen feet by twenty-four. It contains one family room, with ample fire-place and three sleeping rooms. This was the first sample of "clapboard architecture" in the Kirkland patent. In this cottage door he sat, nearly a century ago, on Sabbath evenings in the presence of his swarthy unconverted Bible class, some of whom had walked thirty miles to hear him. The cottage has been removed to the College Campus and is called "The Cradle of Hamilton College." It stands near the entrance to the College Cemetery, in which Kirkland sleeps awaiting the resur-

2

rection of the dead.   Prof. North in an address, thus refers to the
historical cottage :

"After reading the record of Kirkland's life, one can see him
serene and cheerful in the midst of dangers thickest on every side,
with his faith in the power of the Gospel never weakened ; not
when tried for his life on the charge of being a malignant sor-
cerer, not when he sees a musket aimed at his heart by a skulk-
ing savage, not when he wakes up in the morning to find a bloody
tomahawk driven into the door of his cottage.   One can see the
patient missionary skilfully, prayerfully instructing those blood-
thirsty savages by word and example, in peaceful arts of planting
and sowing and reaping, and grafting, and weaving, and building
and reading and writing.   One can see him astutely holding back
those bloodhounds of war when they were eager to league with
the forces of England to exterminate our infant settlements in
Central and Western New York.

In the still hours of the night, we can see him in his lonely cottage, writing long letters on religious topics to good men in Lon-
don and Boston, and other long letters on political and educational
matters to men highest in national and state authority—to President Washington, to General Knox, to Alex. Hamilton, to General Clinton.   When weary with writing, one can see him kneel-
ing by his bedside and gathering new strength where he taught
his dusky disciples to find it by talking with the Great Spirit.
One can see him in his family circle with his open Bible before
him and his bright children about him, one of whom was to be
the first wife of the greatest Bible scholar in America, another
the mother of his gifted biographer, a third most eminent among
the sons and Presidents of Harvard College.   One can see the
gracious simplicity that ennobled the hospitalities of his humble
home, where he receives frequent calls from the Chieftan Schenandoa, from James Dean, the fearless interpreter, from Kunker-
pot, Onondego, Plattkopf, and Samson Occum, the Indian orators;
and those most memorable visits from Gov. Clinton and Baron
Steuben; from Timothy Dwight and Jeremiah Day, after their
long vacation ride on horseback from Yale College.   One can see
him laying out and maturing his plans and large benefactions for
a new seat of Christian learning that shall be to Central New
York what Harvard and Yale and Dartmouth then were to New
England.   When one sees all this, and other kindred sights, as

easy to be seen with fancy's eye, it will not be strange if that unpainted, weather-beaten cottage with its crumbling chimney and narrow windows, swells into a sacred pile, with something of the grandeur and hallowed inspirations of an old cathedral."

Years ago an aged resident of Clinton, Mrs. Eliza Bristol Lucas, now deceased, but the then "remaining link" between the present generation and that which first peopled the Oriskany valley, said that in her girlhood she frequently saw the Indians of the Stockbridge and Oneida tribes go past her father's door, and file up the college-hill road, which was then only an Indian trail. She remembered well how strolling bands of the Indians used to come to her father's house at night-fall in winter, and ask leave to sleep on the kitchen floor. "If

KIRKLAND COTTAGE,
" The Cradle of Hamilton College."

sober, their request was granted. They rolled themselves up in the blankets with their feet towards the fire of logs and after chatting awhile to one another at length dropped off into sleep. They always rose before day-break, and silently went on their way. She remembered seeing troops of Indians loitering around Dominie Kirkland's house, and sometimes sitting on the grass with him and his children. When Schenandoa, the old chief, supposing his end was nigh, came over from Oneida to Clinton, in the hope that he might die there, he was carefully nursed by Mr. Kirkland and his family. Mrs. Lucas remembered one day seeing Miss Eliza Kirkland, (afterwards the wife of the Rev. Dr. Robinson,) brush out Schenandoa's grey locks and bathe his almost sightless eyes."

HAMILTON ONEIDA ACADEMY.

Kirkland died February 27th, 1808, four years before the College was chartered. At his funeral in the village church, an address by Rev. Dr. Asahel S. Norton, (Yale, 1790,) was interpreted to the

Oneida Indians by James Dean, (Dartmouth, 1773.) Years previous to his death he began to mature plans for a system of schools for the education of Indians and white settlers. In a late number of "The Hamilton Review" is an excellent article on the history of the College. The accomplished under-graduate historian says : "Kirkland's plans included the establishment of primary schools in different places, and an academy, centrally located, for the more thorough education of pupils chosen from the primary schools. He visited Philadelphia and laid his plans before the public men there, among whom was Washington, who became deeply interested in the enterprise. The coöperation of the Governor of New York and the Regents of the University was secured, and a charter granted January 31st, 1793. Alexander Hamilton, the Secretary of the Treasury, and Colonel Pickering, then Post-Master General, furnished substantial aid, and the former was one of the trustees named in the petition for incorporation. In honor of him it was called Hamilton Oneida Academy. Mr. Kirkland's efforts did not stop with securing the contributions of others, but he gave liberally of his own substance. In the College Memorial Hall is the original subscription paper, at the head of which is the following : 'Samuel Kirkland, £10.0.0., and fifteen days work, also 300 acres of land for the use and benefit of the Academy to be leased, and the product applied towards the support of an able instructor.' The gifts to the Academy were for the most part in labor and building materials ; but little money was given. Small as these amounts seem now, they represented a great deal of devotion and self sacrifice then."

The site selected for the Academy was on the present campus, between the Chapel and South College, near the "Property Line," which then separated the white settlements from the Indian Territory ; a suitable site, as the Academy was designed for both whites and Indians. "On a sunny and beautiful afternoon, July 1st, 1793, a brilliant and unusual procession moved up the hill. It was a cavalcade of horsemen and fair ladies. In front rode Mr. Kirkland and Major General Baron Frederick William de Steuben, the brave old warrior who had come in our country's hour of trial to discipline her rude soldiery. Near Kirkland and Steuben rode Mr. Kirkland's three daughters, all accomplished riders, together with citizens and invited guests. Their escort was a company of cavalry, well mounted, equipped and caparisoned. The commander was George Whitfield Kirkland. Among those mounted men were some who had mingled in the fight at Oriskany, or had seen Cornwallis surrender at Yorktown." Schenandoa the Indian Chief, was also present, his hair whitened with unmelting snows. With appropriate, and impressive ceremonies Baron de Steuben laid the corner stone of the new edifice, and the Indian Chief assisted in the dedicatory ceremonies. Ninety-three years later the position of the corner stone was determined, and a handsome monument raised over the spot by the class of '86.

HAMILTON ONEIDA ACADEMY.

By the time the foundations were laid and the frame raised the funds were exhausted. For two years it remained in this condition, receiving the epithet, " Kirkland's Folly." " The foxes burrowed in its foundations, the birds built their nests beneath its rafters, and the squirrels, careering up and down the naked timbers, seemed to join in the general derision." But Kirkland was not to be discouraged. With characteristic push, he secured additional funds, the building was enclosed, and a portion fitted up for the use of the school, which was opened in 1797. The building was ninety feet long, thirty-eight feet wide, and three stories high. The school once organized, its reputation was soon established, and pupils flocked in from the surrounding country to take advantage of the opportunities which it offered. " There is no evidence that any Indian youths were educated at the Academy. Their roaming, restless disposition* chafed under the restraints of school,

* The historian assigns as a reason for their not acquiring an Academic Education, " a roaming and restless disposition." Perhaps this should be received as an *ex parte* statement. Possibly they considered an Academic course as many to-day consider a College course—a useless and an expensive luxury. In the autobiography of Benjamin Franklin are found

and the few whom Kirkland adopted into his own family before
the Academy was opened were soon allowed to return to their
tribes. Yet of the large number trained in his primary schools, a
goodly proportion became intelligent and virtuous men. To this
day their descendants, living in a Western State, revere and bless
no name so much as that of Kirkland." One of the converts to
Christianity under his ministry was Good Peter, an Oneida chief.
One Sunday afternoon, when illness prevented Mr. Kirkland from
finishing his sermon, he asked Good Peter to exhort the people.
Peter arose and with much modesty began to address his coun-
trymen upon the great goodness and mercy of God in sending his
only Son to take upon Himself the form of sinful men, and to
suffer and die for their redemption. After depicting the human
life and character of Christ in various aspects, he said, "And yet
he was the great God who created all things; He walked on
earth with men, and had the form of man, but He was all the
while the same Great Spirit; He had only thrown his blanket
around Him."

Although the Oneidas did not avail themselves of the opportunities the Academy afforded them, they held Kirkland in grateful
esteem. His beloved name is cherished not only by their
descendants in the West, but by the remnant of the tribe which
remains on the reservation near Clinton. Recently an Oneida in
the Indian summer-camp at Saratoga Springs said to a Hamilton
graduate, who fell into conversation with him, and spoke of Clinton, "We do not call that Clinton. We call it 'Gar-de-da-wis-

remarks about American Indians. He says, " Our laborious manner of life, compared with
theirs, they esteem slavish and base; and the learning on which we value ourselves they
regard as frivolous and useless. An instance of this occurred at the treaty of Lancaster, in
Pennsylvania, *anno* 1744, between the government of Virginia and the Six Nations. After the
principal business was settled, the commissioners from Virginia acquainted the Indians by
a speech, that there was at Williamsburgh a college, with a fund for educating Indian
youth; and that, if the chiefs of the Six Nations would send down half a dozen of their sons
to that college, the government would take care that they should be well provided for, and
instructed in all the learning of the white people. It is one of the Indian rules of politeness
not to answer a public proposition the same day that it is made: they think that it would be
treating it as a light matter, and they show it respect by taking time to consider it, as of a
matter important. They therefore deferred their answer till the day following, when their
speaker began by expressing their deep sense of the kindness of the Virginia government, in
making them that offer. 'For we know,' says he, 'that you highly esteem the kind of learning
taught in those colleges, and that the maintenance of our young men, while with you, would
be very expensive to you. We are convinced, therefore, that you mean to do us good by your
proposal; and we thank you heartily. But you who are wise must know, that different nations
have different conceptions of things; and you will therefore not take it amiss if our ideas of
this kind of education happen not to be the same with yours. We have had some experience of
it; several of our young people were formerly brought up at colleges of the northern provinces:
they were instructed in all your sciences; but when they came back to us they were bad
runners; ignorant of every means of living in the woods; unable to bear either cold or
hunger; knew neither how to build a cabin, take a deer, or kill an enemy; spoke our
language imperfectly; were therefore neither fit for hunters, warriors or counsellors; they
were totally good for nothing. We are not, however, the less obliged by your kind offer,
though we decline accepting it; and to show our grateful sense of it, if the gentlemen of Virginia will send us a dozen of their sons, we will take great care of their education, instruct
them in all we know, and make men of them.'"

la-ga.'" "What does that mean?" said the Hamiltonian. He replied, "It means the place where the minister lives." Evidently the minister was to their fathers a human angel, and the place is fragrant with the odor of his sanctity. The red Oneida at Saratoga, shaping his bows and arrows, referred also to Hamilton College, but not by that name. The Indians called it, "You-da-te-ci-on-ny-en-ni-ta-go," which means, "The Great School."

PRINCIPALS OF HAMILTON ONEIDA ACADEMY.

The first principal of the Hamilton Oneida Academy was John Niles. He remained there three years when failing health compelled him to withdraw. His associate, the Rev. James Murdock, was afterward called to the Chair of Languages in the University of Vermont, and later became Professor of Church History in Andover Theological Seminary. The Rev. Robert Porter held the principalship for four years, and on February 28th, was succeeded by the Rev. Seth Norton, a thorough scholar, who was retained at the head until the Academy merged into the College. All of these men were graduates of Yale. Professor Norton was the author of both the words and the music of the familiar tune "Devonshire," beginning — "Ye servants of God, your Master proclaim."

GRAVES OF KIRKLAND AND SCHENANDOA.

In 1808, while Seth Norton was principal of the Academy, Kirkland died, lamented by every friend of education and Christianity. He had lived long enough to see the institution he planted enter upon its mission of wide usefulness. Pupils trained within its walls were going forth "to walk conspicuous in the world's light," to preach the gospel and to plead in courts of law. Schenandoa sank into the sleep of death on the 11th of May, 1816, aged about one hundred and ten years. The venerable Oneida, in the twilight of his life said, "I am an aged hemlock. The winds of a hundred winters have whistled through my branches. I am dead at the top." He requested that his grave might be made near Kirkland's. "Bury me beside my white father, so that I may cling to the skirts of his garments, and go up with him at the great resurrection."

Hamilton students standing in the doorway of the Kirkland Cottage see an Indian grave in the College Cemetery. Upon it the shadow of a motionless sentinel, Kirkland's monument, falls like a caress. The loving missionary of the cross and his dusky disciple sleep together. The winds that sweep over the old College halls touch the branches of the elms and poplars, as harp strings are touched, playing through the years requiems for those who rest. The fleecy flakes of four-score winters have softly descended upon their graves, and the leaves of sombre autumns have silently strewn themselves on the sacred sod. Showers of returning springs fall like tears. and still the Christian teacher and the converted chief sleep "the iron sleep." The bright beams of many summer suns have lain across their monuments and kissed the flowers upon their mounds, but Kirkland and Schenandoa do not wake.

> "Sound asleep,
> No sigh can reach them,
> For they dream the heavenly dream;
> No to-morrow's silver speech
> Wakes them with an earthly theme;
> Summer rains relentlessly
> Patter where their heads do lie,
> And the wild flower and the brake
> All their summer leisure take."

When the young scholar buried himself in the forests, his life might have been reckoned by the worldling as lost. But who loses his life for Christ's sake shall find it again. On the resurrection morning, when Kirkland shall rise from that hallowed grave to stand among the redeemed with his Indian disciples, and say, "Here am I and those thou hast given me," who knows but that mingled wonder and happiness shall be his, when it shall be revealed to him how a great host were fitted for life's work and worship in the Christian college he planted. As he receives his crown, radiant with many stars, will he not more fully comprehend the significance of that promise "Them that honor me, I will honor, saith the Lord?"

GEORGE BRISTOL AND MARK HOPKINS.

One of the students in Hamilton Oneida Academy was George Bristol, who continued his studies in Hamilton College and delivered the valedictory oration at the first commencement. He studied law. but his health was so delicate that by the advice of his physician he gave up the practice of law and devoted himself to

PRESIDENTS OF HAMILTON COLLEGE.

1. THE REV. DR. AZEL BACKUS.
3. THE REV. DR. S. E. DWIGHT.
5. THE REV. DR. SIMEON NORTH.
7. THE REV. DR. SAM'L G. BROWN.

2. THE REV. DR. HENRY DAVIS.
4. THE REV. DR. JOSEPH PENNEY.
6. THE REV. DR. SAM'L W. FISHER.
8. THE REV. DR. HENRY DARLING.

agriculture. For one year he taught a classical school in Clinton. Among his pupils was Mark Hopkins, since widely known as the President of Williams College. It was he of whom President Garfield said, "Place Mark Hopkins at one end of a bench and a student at the other and you have a college." "God bless the dear old Doctor!" True it is, indeed, that neither stone nor timber nor mastercraft of builders, but men, constitute a commonwealth or college. As the editor of the Alumniana, in the "Hamilton Literary Monthly," writes:

Οὐ λίθοι, οὐδὲ ξύλα, οὐδὲ
τέχνη τεκτόνων αἱ πόλεις εἰσιν,
ἀλλ᾽ ὅπουπερ ἂν ὦσιν 'ΑΝΔΡΕΣ
αὑτοὺς σώζειν εἰδότες,
ἐνταῦθα τείχη καὶ πόλεις.

THE COLLEGE CHARTERED.

"As the demands upon Hamilton Oneida Academy grew, the necessity of increasing its facilities and enlarging its field of usefulness became imperative. Its proximity to the "Old Seneca Turnpike," (a former Indian trail twelve or eighteen inches wide, and extending across the State, and later the main thoroughfare from Albany to Buffalo,) which passed through the present village of Kirkland, made it a convenient location for a college. A subscription was again opened to secure the endowment of a college. It was necessary to raise Fifty Thousand Dollars in order to obtain a charter and secure an additional Fifty Thousand Dollars as a grant from the State. The work of soliciting subscriptions was committed to the Rev. Caleb Alexander, (Yale 1777,) who in a few months secured the necessary funds. The patroon of Albany, Stephen Van Rensselaer, headed the subscription with One Thousand Dollars, and Daniel T. Tompkins, the Governor of the State, and afterwards Vice-President of the United States, gave five hundred dollars. May 26th, 1812, the Regents of the University granted a charter to Hamilton College. By direction of the Trustees the unfinished Academy building was completed and such additions made as the new institution required."

PRESIDENT BACKUS.

The College has had eight Presidents. The Rev. Dr. Azel Backus, an alumnus of Yale, presided from 1812 to 1816, the year of his death. He was inaugurated in the village church, December 3rd, 1812. Professor Seth Norton delivered on the occasion a Latin address. Dr. Backus was an earnest and eloquent preacher of the Gospel. His mental characteristics, for he was by turns pathetic and humorous, furnish evidence to support the theory that pathos and humor are "twin sisters." "The partition between tears and smiles is very thin." Twenty years ago, at an alumni meeting in New York City, an eminent graduate, Judge Charles P. Kirkland, LL. D., class of 1816, said: "Dr. Backus was a man of genius and of the most kindly feelings. He never preached to us without tears, nor censured a student without deep emotion. He disliked above all things attempts at 'fine writing,' and on one occasion, when one of my classmates read for his composition a colloquy brilliant with wit, as he supposed, the President's sole criticism was: 'There's no Attic salt in that; nothing but shad brine.' The author of that colloquy became a distinguished citizen of the state in which he resided." Perhaps it is the genial influence of good Dr. Backus, which has pervaded from the beginning those college halls, repeatedly awakening their echoes with genuine wit. Perchance one of the college poets was under the spell of that influence, when he wrote the

BACCHANAL BALLAD.

AIR—"LITORIA."

I.

Prex Backus was a jovial Prex,
The roughest, kindest of his sex,
His lips let fly full many a joke,
And jests he woke that others spoke.

II.

One night he caught a Freshman tight,
And helped him home with wrath and might;
In other words a Freshman drunk
He shouldered like a traveler's trunk.

III.

The Freshman's plucky _Mater_ wit
Gave back this saucy saving hit—
" _O quo me, Bacche, plenum te,_
O magne Prex, quo rapis me ?"

IV.

When the tired Teacher shuts his book,
When Pastors rest, by hook or crook,
When city Bankers seek to know
A bank whereon wild violets grow;

V.

When Doctors, Lawyers, Editors,
Would sharpen up their ancient saws,
When half a century's uncorked wit
Floods the gay board where Brothers sit,

VI.

And, drunk with frolic, titled men
Grow back to College Boys again,
Then good Prex Backus' jovial soul
Fills up for each the brimming bowl;

VII.

Each Mother's Son grasps by the hand,
And wrings from each the old demand,
" *O quo me Bacche, plenum te,*
O magne Prex, quo rapis me."

HON. GERRIT SMITH AND THE REV. DR. EDW. ROBINSON.

One of the students in college during the administration of Dr. Backus was Gerrit Smith, afterward known so widely as the American philanthropist. His first wife was the only daughter of Dr. Backus.

Another brilliant gem was set in the crown encircling Hamilton's brow during the administration of the first President. The name, Edward Robinson, awakens gratitude in the hearts of scholars in all lands. He graduated at Hamilton in 1816. His birth place was Southington, Conn. In an address delivered there several years ago, the Rev. Dr. Upson said : " In counting our family jewels to-day we are all proud of the name of Edward Robinson. I need not tell you that he was a very remarkable man. Of stalwart frame, he was as energetic and industrious and persevering, as he was physically strong. An indomitable traveller, he was a most determined searcher after geographical truth. His knowledge was extensive in all departments. He was as exact and minute as a German scholar. In all directions he had the Teutonic spirit. His name cannot be forgotten. It is identified with the Holy Land. No modern history of the holy places can be written, which shall not mention his name.

The Bible will perpetuate his fame. Those who shed light upon Biblical record have to be remembered." Dean Stanley once said, " Dr. Robinson was the first man who saw Palestine with his eyes open to what he ought to see."

He served Hamilton College as tutor during 1817–18, and then engaged in private study of the Greek classics until 1821, when he went to Andover, Mass., in order to publish an edition of the Iliad. In 1826 he went to Europe where he studied Hebrew under Gesenius at Halle, and also history under Neander. In 1830 he was called to Andover as professor extraordinary of Biblical Literature, and entered with enthusiasm upon the work of instruction and the publication of scholarly works upon the Bible. In 1831 he founded the Biblical Repository, a theological review, which introduced a new era in theological periodicals in America, and which subsequently passed over into the Bibliotheca Sacra. He was the author of many books, among them a Greek and English Lexicon of the New Testament, and a translation of Gesenius' Hebrew Lexicon. In 1837 he was called to the professorship of Biblical literature in Union Theological Seminary, New York. He accepted the call upon condition that he should receive leave of absence some years in order to explore the lands of the Bible. Upon his return he published Biblical Researches in three volumes simultaneously in Berlin and Boston. He died in New York City on Jan. 27th, 1863. A volume on the Life, Writings and Character of that eminent scholar was published by the Rev. Dr. Henry B. Smith and President Roswell D. Hitchcock of Union Seminary. Dr. Robinson's valuable library is the property of Hamilton College.

FUNERAL OF SCHENANDOA.

The funeral services of Schenandoa, the aged Indian chief, were held in Clinton, while Dr. Backus presided over the college. They were largely attended by white people and Indians, many of the latter coming from Oneida for that purpose. An eye-witness relates that the Indians, men and women, were seated in the middle pews of the church, and the whites in the other seats, and in the galleries. Rev. Dr. Backus, made an address to the Indians, which Judge James Dean, (Dartmouth, 1773), the Indian agent, standing beneath the pulpit, interpreted. " The Indians rose to their feet during the address. If Indian stoicism forbade tears and loud lamentations, doubtless every heart mourned for the brave old chief with ingenuous sorrow. After prayer and the singing of appropriate hymns, the body was carried to the grave, the order of the procession being as follows: First, students of the College; next, the hearse, followed by the Indians; and behind these Mrs. Kirkland and family, Judge Dean, Rev. Dr. Norton, Rev. Mr. Ayres, President Backus and other officers of the college, and citizens. The remains were borne to the garden of Mr. Kirkland, where they were buried according to his desire. In the year 1856, by authority of the trustees of the College, the body of Rev. Mr. Kirkland, together with that of Schenandoa, was disinterred and removed to the College cemetery.

DEATH OF PRESIDENT BACKUS.

The Rev. Dr. Backus died December 28th, 1816, and his grave is in the College Cemetery. The epitaph on his monument is:

H. S. E.

AZEL BACKUS. S. T. D.
VIR PIETATE INSIGNIS, OMNI DOCTRINA
EXCULTUS, EVANGELII MINISTER
FERVIDUS ET PRÆCLARUS. COLLEGII
HAMILTONENSIS FUIT PRÆSES;
SEMPER DILIGENTISSIMUS, ET
ALUMNIS CARISSIMUS. IN EO SUMMA
IN HOMINES BENEVOLENTIA, MISERI
CORDIA, INCORRUPTA FIDES,
NUDAQUE VERITAS. CONJUX
SUPERSTES DOLET; FILII ET FILIA
GEMUNT, ET OMNES QUIBUS
VIVENS ILLE FUIT NOTUS,
LUGENT ET PLORANT.

(Reverse.)

MEMORIE PRÆSIDIS DILECTISSIMI
ET VENERANDI, CURATORES
COLLEGII HAMILTONENSIS HOC
MONUMENTUM POSUERUNT.

———

ECCLESIÆ APUD BETHLEM,
CONN. PASTOR
ANNOS XXII.
COLL. HAM. PRÆSES
IV.
DE VITA DECESSIT
DIE DEC. DUODETRICESIMO,
ANNO DOMINI MDCCCXVI,
ÆT. LII.

PRESIDENT DAVIS.

The second President of Hamilton was the Rev. Dr. Henry Davis, a graduate of Yale, who as tutor, had rendered service to Williams and Yale, and as professor of languages to Union. He was President of Middlebury College, Vermont, when he was called to the Presidency of Yale and of Hamilton. He accepted the call to Hamilton, and presided over the College from 1817 to 1833. Dr. Davis' scholarship was thorough, and his love of letters and the church was great. He was active in establishing Auburn Theological Seminary, and the American Board of Commissioners for Foreign Missions.

An event, as unique as it was interesting, occurred during Dr. Davis' presidency. It was on the occasion of the erection of a monument to the memory of Schenandoa by the Northern Missionary Society. "On a dark and cold and cloudy day in November or December, 1819, a large audience assembled in the College cemetery; the Oneidas, men and women, from one to two hundred strong, came from their homes clothed in their native costume. Rev. Arthur J. Stansbury, of Albany, delivered a dedicatory address, which was interpreted to the Indians, sentence by sentence, by the minister of their church. These ceremonies closed, the sons and daughters of the forest took up their march to Oneida, and the College community and the citizens of the town listened in the village church to an eloquent sermon from Mr. Stansbury."

PRESIDENT DWIGHT.

The successor of the Rev. Dr. Davis was the Rev. Dr. Sereno Edwards Dwight, the son of President Timothy Dwight, of Yale. After graduating at New Haven he studied law and subsequently theology. He was Chaplain of the United States Senate, and in 1817 was pastor of Park Street Church, Boston, where he remained ten years. Ill health obliged him to resign, and returning to New Haven, he occupied himself in writing the life and editing the works of the elder Edwards, which were published in 1829. In 1828, in connection with his brother Henry, he opened in New Haven a school on the plan of the German gymnasium. In March, 1833, he was chosen President of Hamilton College, but resigned in 1835 on account of ill health.

PRESIDENT PENNEY.

The Rev. Dr. Joseph Penney, who studied at Trinity College, Dublin, and finished his University education at Glasgow in 1813, was the fourth President of the College. He brought to the service of Hamilton accurate scholarship and fine pulpit ability. In 1839 he resigned.

PRESIDENT NORTH.

The Rev. Dr. Simeon North, who was valedictorian of the class of 1825, Yale College, succeeded Dr. Penney. He occupied the Chair of Languages in Hamilton ten years before he was called to the Presidency. He presided eighteen years and during his administration the Institution enjoyed great prosperity.

The Hon. Theodore W. Dwight, LL. D., Warden of Columbia College Law School, paid this tribute to President North: " I knew Dr. North well. I was a student under him for three years, was for sixteen years a member of the faculty, then was associated with him as a college trustee. My acquaintance with him commenced nearly fifty years ago, and was continued until his death.

The quality that struck me most in my acquaintance with him was accurate, profound, and earnest scholarship. In all his manifold work he stands out before me most clearly as a professor of Greek. Having myself in early life a passionate love for Greek, I found in him one who could fully satisfy my desires. The academic instruction of that time was not very thorough, so far at least as it was accessible to the men I knew. It rather tended towards fluency of translation than to thoroughness of scholarship and critical study. Dr. North set himself resolutely against this tendency. No student could win his favor in a high degree, who did not appreciate the niceties of construction, and the force of those expressive particles which add so much to the beauty and strength of the Greek language. At the same time, he was alive to the poetic or literary sentiment, the ineffable charm and grace of style and diction of the great authors, on whose works he commented. He led the most reluctant student along the most difficult paths of his department with a winning and persuasive manner which awakened interest, even where it did not arouse enthusiasm.

I recall an instance of this happy method. As long ago as 1839,

the college authorities established for a short period elective studies, now so prevalent. Four of the class to which I belonged
elected Greek. When we asked him for our text book he said
with a genial smile that we would have 'Longinus on the Sub-
lime.' We were completely disconcerted, for Longinus had the
reputation of being the most difficult Greek known to modern
man. This occurred before the day of accessible translations. It
implied the hardest kind of mental labor. He was, however, so
earnest, so eager that we should understand it, so capable in
explanation, and so successful in exposition, that the dreaded
book became a delight, and to the present moment 'Longinus' is
the Greek word to which the memory recurs with special pleasure.
Had Dr. North continued in the Chair of Greek, he would have
left a great name among the accomplished scholars of our time in
their special department of study, which in spite of all modern
attack, has for ages been, and will continue to be, the most potent
instrumentality for the development of mental force and literary
grace.

A marked feature of his character was a perfect kindliness of
spirit and charm of manner. He was a thorough gentleman.
Meeting him almost daily for so many years, and sometimes on
occasions that would try one's temper, I never heard an ill-natured
word, nor saw the slightest evidence of temper—not even impa-
tience. His winning smile, which on due occasions would develop
into a joyous laugh, disclosed the uniform, kindly quality of his
nature. After he left the professorship for the presidency, he held
a delicate and most difficult position. The presidency of a college like Hamilton is a far more trying place than that of a larger
institution like Yale or Harvard. The president is but one of a
number of officers. He has no veto power. His vote counts
for no more than that of his humblest associate. He must frequently submit to a line of policy which his judgment condemns.
Yet the public, not appreciating the situation, will hold him
responsible for the failure of a course of action thus forced
upon him by his associates. In a larger institution the burden
of administration does not rest upon the president alone, but is
shared with others. A president at Hamilton thus needs a true
equilibrium of qualities. Kindness, firmness, patience in listening, promptness in action, willingness to take on the necessary
responsibility, cautiousness and conservatism, must be so exquis-

itely blended as to produce a symmetrical and successful administration. Who shall possess these qualities in such proportion as
never to err in excess or deficiency? No one. Perfect success is
impossible. An approximation to it only can be expected. The
administration of Dr. North was criticised in some quarters,
because it was said to exhibit kindness of feeling at the expense
of force. I confess that at the time I shared, to some extent, in
this criticism. Later experience and reflection have largely
modified these views. Kindness of spirit, nay, an affectionate
disposition towards the students on the part of the college officers,
will be in the future the predominating feature in the government
of an American college. The reciprocal affection and respect on
the part of the students thus generated, is the true source of gov-
ernmental power. A wise and able man will not allow, on this
account, government to degenerate into laxness. On the other
hand, he will use the influence he thus obtains as the instrument
of a firmer administration.

Combining the qualities of President North in my memory, I
think that he unites, in an uncommon degree, what Matthew
Arnold has made so familiar to us by the expression, ·Sweetness
and light.' There was in him an abundance of culture and ripe
scholarship, softened by gentleness of disposition and a profound
regard for the feelings and interests of others. His intellect
illuminated his sentiments, while his affections lent grace to his
masculine understanding.

Another very strong element in President North's character,
was his interest in young men, particularly in his former
students. Few of these did he ever forget or fail to watch their
future career with an affectionate interest. Before the age of
sixty he retired from active life, as the poet of old, to his ·Sabine
Farm,' where from his quiet outlook he studied the affairs of the
world with an absorbing and philosophical interest. Whenever I
met with him in later years, I was surprised at the extent and
accuracy of his knowledge of current affairs. He was particularly
familiar with the achievements of his students in their later years,
and referred to them in conversation with interest and high satisfaction, even though his acquaintance with them dated far back
into his early life.

I believe that there is no man living in Oneida County, who com-
bines the leading characteristics of President North, regard bein·

had to his thorough and wide classical scholarship, excellence of literary style, vigor of expression, sweetness of disposition, affectionate nature, genuine modesty, with an accompanying tendency to withdraw from public observation, sound judgment, wise cautiousness, tranquil wisdom, and an intelligent Christian faith, based on the Puritan creed of his ancestry. It is in no ordinary sense true that his departure has left a vacancy which will not be filled, and which those who knew him will not cease to regret.

Farewell, gentle, kind, and manly nature : in the world, but not of it ; the elevated hillside in Kirkland, sloping toward the east, withdrawn from the clang and bustle of business, and yet a quiet and comprehensive outpost of observation of it, is a reminder of your appropriate resting place !'"

Daniel Huntington, LL. D., President of the American Academy of Design, also laid a wreath upon the grave of President North. He said, "I loved and revered Rev. Dr. North deeply. He treated me as kindly and tenderly and generously as though I had been his son. But for his thoughtful, affectionate treatment while I was a Sophomore on College Hill, I should undoubtedly have been suspended. He saw my passion for painting, how it was absorbing my thoughts and distracting my mind from study, and secured for me an honorable commendation to the Art Department of the University of the City of New York, then under the direction of Professor S. F. B. Morse. Professor Lathrop joined with him in this kind consideration. I remember the Elliott portrait of Dr. North very well, and that I attempted to copy it, but of course it was quite beyond me. The Half-Century Letter* of the class of 1833, by Thomas W. Seward, is a racy performance, and recalls the wit, and genial humor of his brother, Alexander Seward, whom I well knew.

Judge Dwight's article on President North is very interesting, and expresses with great force and beauty the wonderful variety of traits which were united in his character."

A characteristic testimonial to President North's personal influence was given by Henry W. Shaw, better known in the newspapers as "Josh Billings," who did not graduate, but was for

*The historian, who shall undertake to write a comprehensive history of Hamilton College will greatly value the Half-Century Letters. If published, they would make a very interesting volume. The "Letter" of the class of 1833, to which reference is here made, recalled the coming to Clinton of the gifted and handsome young portrait-painter, (Elliott,) his popularity with the collegians, and his marked influence upon the student Huntington, "an infant brother in art, whose steps he first guided in the path since trodden with so great renown."

several years a student in the college. When he was asked how he managed to climb up and down the chapel lightning-rod without breaking his sophomoric neck, his solemn visage lighted up with a cheerful reply, " So you, too, have been at Hamilton College. You see, I was full of the devil there, that was what was the matter with me. There was a Greek and Latin man in the Faculty, who had studied Socrates to some purpose. He didn't go to work to kill the boy and leave the devil. His plan was just contrary to that, to kill off the devil and leave the boy."

During President North's administration, the Rev. Dr. Henry Mandeville was called to the Chair of Moral Philosophy and Rhetoric. He wrote at Hamilton his system of Elocution, " basing it upon the principle enunicated by Walker, that the structure of a sentence should control its delivery—the only true, philosophical idea of a sound elocution." Mandeville was enthusiastic. He made his students enthusiastic.

PRESIDENT FISHER.

The Rev. Dr. Samuel Ware Fisher, also a Yale alumnus, was the successor of President North. His commanding eloquence and administrative ability widened the reputation of the College.

He was earnest in giving the Bible a prominent place in the Hamilton College curriculum. He regarded it as the book of the great King and the great king of books, its pages fragrant with the odor of sanctity and luminous with the smile of God. To be deeply read in the oracles of God he esteemed of vast import-ance. At his inaugural he said :

" Shall we, having charge of youth in the very years when they are most impressible, shall we not induct them thoroughly into these thoughts, these facts, this grand system taught in the Scrip-tures? Shall we deem our duty done when we have read a daily chapter, and preached a weekly sermon, and lectured a few times on some of the evidences of its inspiration? Shall we be wiser for time than we are for eternity, and train up youth richer in pagan than in Christian lore? The Bible is the heart, the sun of a truly Christian education. And how shall we educate men as Christians, how shall we ground them effectually in that which constitutes Christianity, unless we do for them what Cicero would have done for educated Roman youth, in respect to the twelve tables—make it the *carmen necessarium* of an educated American!

If he could say that the 'twelve tables were worth more than all the libraries of the philosopher,' and therefore should be studied more constantly and profoundly, may we not, with equal truth, affirm that the Bible is worth more than all philosophy, all natural science, all other forms of thought; and, therefore, it should be of all books the most profoundly studied, the most constantly present through the whole process of education? We would place the Bible in the hands of the youth, when first, with a trembling heart and heightened expectation, he enters these halls. We would make it his study, his companion from week to week, as his mind opens and his powers of reflection expand. We would have this light shed its steady, serene brightness all along his ascending way until he goes forth alone into the stern conflict of life. We would have no compromise with infidelity of skepticism, on this subject; we are Christian educators: we pride God's word above all earthly science. There is our banner—we fling it to the breeze! If you send your son hither, we shall do all that in us lies to teach him what this book contains, and to make its truths effective in the control of his life. We shall not apologize for Christianity, nor treat it as a hand-maid to natural science, but as the queen-regent over all our studies, our lives, our richest posession in time, our only hope for eternity.

The Bible is not to be taught from the stand-point of mere literature. It is not as a human inspiration, but as a divine revelation, it occupies this chief seat in an institution of learning. I will not degrade it from this position by studying it as if it were the songs of Homer, or the *De Corona* of Demosthenes, or the history of Thucydides. It is not because it has the oldest history, the sublimest poetry, the most touching stories, the most compact reasoning, the richest figures of rhetoric, that it is worthy to be the *vade-mecum* of our youth; it is *as a divine revelation*, thrilling through all its nervous words with the inspiration of Jehovah; opening to man the will of his Maker in its unmistakable purity; ministering to the wants of a soul diseased, and an intellect benighted, swelling in a broad tide with divine compassion, and designed to lift men from the troublous depths of earthly pollution, sorrow and death-darkness, into the purity, the joy, and the light of a new light in Christ Jesus:—as a revelation it claims the student's daily attention and challenges his profoundest thought.

From this stand-point of an assured divine revelation respecting our duties and our hopes, I would teach the Bible.

I would also secure the constant study of the Bible by making proficiency in the knowledge of it enter into the final estimate of the character and standing of the scholar. In this respect, it should occupy the same position in the college curriculum as any other study. Instead of being left to the caprice of the student to be engaged in or not as he may choose, it should be enforced precisely as is the study of the classics or mathematics.

The *influence* of this study will at once vindicate the position assigned to it in the system of collegiate education. Its direct effect upon the intellect, in invigorating all its powers, is great. It also places the student in a position where he is better prepared to see and fairly judge of the harmony of the entire circle of science. No man can approximate to the completeness of general scholarship without having studied profoundly its great system of truth. It is in the light of the celestial we shall see more justly the terrestrial. . . . . Another result is the solid basis which it lays for an intelligent faith in the Bible as a divine revelation. Ignorance is the great enemy of the Christian faith. To send forth into the world a young man, thoroughly at home in material and secular knowledge, but imperfectly grounded in that which is of vaster importance and profounder influence upon himself and society, is frequently to do both him and Christianity an incalculable injury.

But besides all this, we need this divine word as a most effective influence for direct and moral religious culture. Intellectual convictions are indeed of incalculable importance; but unless these convictions have entered the heart, so as to become principles of action, education has not accomplished its greatest work. The higher nature of man lies deeper in the soul. From the secret depths where thought becomes emotion and conviction principle, the influences arise that constitute character. This is the richest field of culture; this demands the profoundest wisdom, the most patient effort, on the part of the instructor. It is with respect to this, more than all other departments of his work he feels his weakness. He may form the intellect, but how shall he reach, control, and give a noble character to the secret impulses and purposes? How shall he get access to that heart, chasten its affections, discipline its eager desires; subdue its wild passions, waken it to high and holy aspirations? It is here he feels the need of that which is divine: here he must call to his aid influences profound as the nature, and mightier than the passions of the soul."

President Fisher, as an expounder of Scripture and a preacher of the everlasting Gospel, especially attracted men of trained minds and thoughtful habit. "When roused by strong emotion he would pour forth from a full mind and warm heart a tide of eloquent speech that bore his hearers away as with the sweep and rush of mighty waters." After rendering the college efficient service as President from 1858 to 1866, Dr. Fisher resigned, and on November 15th, 1867, was installed Pastor of Westminster Church, Utica, New York. He died in Cincinnati, Ohio, January 18th, 1874.

PRESIDENT BROWN.

In 1867, the Rev. Dr. Samuel Gilman Brown, a son of President Brown of Dartmouth, accepted the Presidency of Hamilton. He had occupied at Dartmouth the Chair of Oratory and Belles-Lettres, also of Intellectual Philosophy and Political Economy. He was President of Hamilton from 1867 to 1881. Subsequently for a while he filled his former chair at Dartmouth and for two years he gave instruction in Mental and Moral Philosophy to the seniors in Bowdoin College.

Both in letters and in his pulpit ministrations, President Brown was eminent. His pen traced sentences classic in their beauty, and his cultured voice pronounced periods finished and effective. When his death, which occurred November 4th, 1885, was announced, three colleges—Hamilton, Dartmouth, and Bowdoin,—together with various literary and religious societies, paid tender tributes to his memory. In a memorial presented by President Hitchcock, of Union Theological Seminary, and adopted by Chi Alpha, an Association of New York ministers, Dr. Brown is portrayed as an accurate scholar, an admirable teacher of catholic judgment, unerring taste, fine, gracious manners, and lofty Christian purpose. Senator Hawley said at an alumni reunion; "It has not been my fortune to come into contact with a sweeter Christian spirit." Dr. North writes of President Brown; "He will be enrolled in the list of prominent Americans as one whose profound and accurate learning was a power without pedantry and ostentation, whose intellectual strength was a sword wreathed in myrtle, whose home-life was as beautiful and sweet as his public career was honorably useful and blameless." The Rev. Dr. Isaac S. Hartley, of Utica, said: "His extensive and varied reading, his close and exhaustive study, his knowledge of philosophy and familiarity with the teachings of the schools made him quick and ready in thought, while his scholarly taste, united with a faultless style, brought that thought to you, clothed in the richest, yet simplest apparel . . . . Themes social, economic, and philanthropic, found in him also a student; and whenever alluded to he discussed them with unusual fluency, his words ever revealing previous reflection, as well as the possession of the calm, judicial mind . . . . . But the subject to which, perhaps, he most frequently reverted in these hours by the way, as well as when surrounded with his more intimate friends, was Christianity and its influence; what it had wrought and what it was working, and what he believed it would some day include in its holy grasp. With him it was no mere creed or set of defined doctrines, but a life, a force —and a divine life and force. In the ministerial meeting his presence was anxiously looked for, and when he spoke on the question under discussion, his wisdom, humility and sweetness of spirit wooed and won."

THE KIRKLAND MONUMENT.

It was during the administration of President Brown that a new monument was dedicated to the memory of the Rev. Samuel Kirkland. A number of the descendants and relatives of Mr. Kirkland were present. Four venerable and highly respected gentlemen— Mr. George Bristol, Mr. John Thompson, Mr. Gaius Butler and Mr. John C. Hastings—who more than sixty years before had been students in Hamilton Oneida Academy, were also in attendance. Twenty or more Indians from the neighborhood of Oneida Castle were also present by invitation, and took part in the exercises. Among them were Daniel Schenandoa and Thomas Schenandoa, the first a Grand Sachem of the Oneidas, and the second a priest, and both of them great-grandsons of the distinguished chief of Mr. Kirkland's time. A graduate of the college, who was scanning with interest a group of copper-colored Oneidas under the shade trees in front of South College, before the formal exercises began, saw Ex-Governor Seymour walk from the college chapel toward South College. He was accompanied by a young man. When they reached the Indians, Governor Seymour beckoned to one of them, and when he had approached him, the Governor said: "Schenandoa, I have the great pleasure of introducing you to Mr. Kirkland, the great-grandson of the Rev. Samuel Kirkland, under whose preaching your great-grandfather became a Christian."

At half-past three o'clock a procession was formed in front of the College chapel in the following order:

1. Marshal of the Day.
2. Gilmore's Band.
3. Undergraduates—first, Class of 1876; second, Class of 1875; third, Class of 1874; fourth, Class of 1873.
4. Trustees of Hamilton College.
5. Descendants and Relatives of Samuel Kirkland.
6. Oneida Indians.
7. Alumni of Hamilton Oneida Academy.
8. Faculty of the College.
9. Alumni of Hamilton and other Colleges in the order of their classes.
10. Citizens.

The procession marched to an open space in the cemetery near the new monument and that of President Backus, where a platform had been erected for the proposed services. On the south side of this platform was suspended a portrait of Rev. Mr. Kirkland from Memorial Hall, and the original subscription for the building of Hamilton Oneida Academy. The platform was occupied by the Trustees and Faculty of the College, the speakers of the day, the descendants of Mr. Kirkland, a portion of the Indians from Oneida, and the surviving students of Hamilton Oneida Academy. In the centre of the stage was a large arm chair, once owned by Mr. Kirkland, and on a table near, his family Bible. The chair is now in Memorial Hall. The Bible is there also, having been presented to the College by A. Norton Brockway, M. D., Class of '57, and now a Trustee of Hamilton. The Bible formerly belonged to Rev. Asahel Strong Norton, the grandfather of Dr. Brockway. The Rev. Dr. Norton was for many years the intimate friend of Kirkland and for twenty-one years a Trustee of the College. The sacred volume was presented to him by Kirkland. The Rev. Dr. A. J. Upson, of Albany, read from this Bible a portion of the 91st Psalm and a portion of the 60th chapter of Isaiah. Prayer was offered by the Rev. Dr. Frank F. Ellinwood, after which an interesting letter was read from the Hon. Charles P. Kirkland, of New York, a grand-nephew of Samuel Kirkland.

The published report of the exercises includes an address by President Brown, a historical address of great interest by Hon. O. S. Williams, an eloquent address by Hon. Horatio Seymour and remarks by Dr. Woolworth, of Albany, who brought with him from the State Library a manuscript volume, which contains two diaries of Samuel Kirkland. Dr. Woolworth also held in his hand the charter of Hamilton Oneida Academy, which is dated "January 31st, the seventeenth year of American Independence."

INDIAN ORATORY.

When Dr. Woolworth had finished his remarks President Brown extended welcome to the Oneida Indians present. He introduced to the audience Thomas Schenandoa and Daniel Schenandoa, both of whom spoke in their native language and were interpreted at short intervals, for the benefit of the assembly, by an Indian interpreter. Rev. Daniel Moose, missionary to the Oneidas, then read a paper embodying the substance of the two Indian speeches. It was as follows:

"Brothers: We have come from our homes to join hands with you to do honor to the memory of a friend of our forefathers.

He was sent by the Good Spirit to teach the Indians to be good and happy. As the sun cometh in the early morning, so he came from the east in 1766, to gladden the hearts of my people and to cover them with the light of the Great Spirit. He came in and went out before them; he walked hand in hand with the Great Schenandoa.

As Kirkland was the counselor, the physician, the spiritual father and friend, so was Schenandoa, like the tall hemlock, the glory of our people, the mighty Sachem and counselor of the Iroquois, and the true friend of the white man. His soul was a beam of fire, his heart was big with goodness, his head was like a clear lamp and his tongue was great in council. Kirkland was to my nation like a great light in a dark place. His soul was like the sun, without any dark spots upon it, and we first learned through him to be good. Our fathers then gave him much land, and he gave to your children Hamilton Oneida Academy.

Where to-day are Kirkland and Schenandoa? They are gone! The Great Spirit reached out of his window and took them from us, and we see them no more. When sixty-nine snows had fallen and melted away, then the good Kirkland went to his long home. At the age of one hundred and ten we laid beside him John Schenendoa, the great Sachem of the Iroquois. Arm in arm as brothers, they walked life's trail; and united in death, nothing can separate them; but they will go up together in the great resurrection.

When they went down to their long sleep the night was dark; when the morning came it did not remove the darkness from our people. They wet their eyes with big drops and a heavy cloud was on them.

The council fires of the Iroquois died, and their hearts grew faint; then our people scattered like frightened deer, and we Indians here to-day, standing by the mighty dead, are the only few of the once powerful Iroquois. They all are gone, but the deeds of Kirkland and Schenandoa will never die; their memory is dear to us and will not fail. So long as the sun lights the sky by day and the moon by night we will rub the mould and dust from their gravestones and say: 'Brothers, here sleep the good and the brave.'"

At the close of this address, a company of Indians, men and women, stepped upon the platform, and sang an anthem in the tongue, wherein they were born, whose simple, plaintive tones touched all hearts. The exercises were then concluded with the benediction by the Rev. Dr. Henry Kendall.

PRESIDENT DARLING'S INAUGURATION.

The Rev. Dr. Henry Darling, who is now the President of the College, is a graduate of Amherst. He was inaugurated September 15th, 1881. After music by the Utica Philharmonic Orchestra, selections from the Scriptures by the Rev. Dr. Samuel H. Gridley, and a prayer by the Rev. Dr. Samuel G. Brown, the Hon. Wm. J. Bacon, LL. D., of the Board of Trustees, delivered the following address.

HON. WILLIAM J. BACON'S ADDRESS.

The duty assigned to me in the services of this day, is one from which I might well have asked to be excused. It fell much more naturally and appropriately to other hands, and belonged, by an original designation, the propriety of which was most readily recognized, to the chairman of the Board of Trustees, that highly honored and gifted man, that profound jurist, and wise and able counselor of the board, Hon. Henry A. Foster. Although he has measured more than four score years, he still moves among us with physical powers but moderately if at all impaired, and in the full strength of his imperial intellect. How great a satisfaction it would have been to us all to have listened to his address of induction and his hearty words of welcome to our incoming President, it would be quite superfluous for me to say. It grieves me to add that a painful domestic bereavement, in which we all deeply sympathize, as we do with our associate and brother, Dr. Kendall, in the sad calamity which has befallen him in the sudden and unexpected loss of his gifted son, deprives us this day I fear of the pleasure of welcoming the presence of either at this important and interesting event in the history of our college.

May He whose office especially and peculiarly it is, to minister to the afflicted and pour the oil of joy into wounded hearts, be to each of them a Son of consolation, and in an emphatic sense "the shadow of a great rock in a weary land."

We have assembled this day, my friends and fellow-citizens, to induct into his high and responsible office, the eighth President of Hamilton College. It is an occasion of deep interest to all her sons here or elsewhere, and to this community an event of no ordinary importance. We meet, too, under circumstances of unusual interest and solemnity. It was pertinently remarked by President Fisher, in the admirable address delivered by him at the jubilee celebration in 1862, that the time of the founding of our college was one most memorable in history. It was in 1812, after the great Revolution had passed which established us as a nation and started us forth on our great mission as a free and united republic, but still "it was amidst the smoke and thunder of war with one of the mightiest of the European powers, that the foundations of the college were laid."

How deeply momentous and profoundly solemn is this moment in which we are standing here. For many weary days and weeks we have been almost breathlessly waiting beneath the deep shadow of impending death, and the whole nation has been watching with an intensity of interest that language can not describe, by the bedside of the illustrious sufferer, who with fortitude unequaled and unapproached save by the one who has also stood by his side, the equally brave, self-sustained and faithful wife, who with a breaking heart has worn a cheerful face, has been battling for life. From that bed of pain what lessons of courage, confidence and faith have been sent forth to all the people of this land. If he conquers in this strife, as God grant he may, what a chorus of grateful praise and thanksgiving will go up to heaven from the heart of the whole united nation.*

Neither the necessities nor the proprieties of this occasion demand from me any discussion of the principles of that higher education which it has been the aim of the authorities of this institution to introduce as an important and essential part of its curriculum. This theme has been largely and well discussed elsewhere, and doubtless will be again; nor yet is it my province to dwell upon what may be deemed the new departure that is contemplated, and from which so much has been promised and so much is expected. It has been intimated to me by one whose slightest suggestion has to me almost the force of authoritative law, that as this address of induction has now for the first time in our history fallen to the lot of an alumnus of the college, and one, too, who had a personal acquaintance with each of the preceding seven presidents of Hamilton, "why," to use his own words, "should not that address include sketches of those seven presidents from Dr. Backus downward!"

Why not, indeed? For several reasons, any one of which might well answer. In the first place, grateful as the theme might be, neither the limited time granted to me, nor the material just now at hand are sufficient for the purpose. In the second place, that

---

*Within four days after the utterance of the above sentiment, it pleased God by a sudden and at the moment a most unexpected stroke, before which we were dumb, and which it is not our province to question or interpret, to remove President Garfield from the scene of his earthly activities to the repose of the grave. Let us not murmur nor vainly ask why was this, but submit all to that ordering of human affairs which only infinite knowledge can comprehend and infinite wisdom and goodness justify.

I desire, however, in brief words, to express my belief that few greater, wiser or better men have ever occupied the high seats of power in our country. He came to the chief magistracy more fully equipped for its duties than any of his predecessors, with possibly a single exception. As a parliamentary debater I think he had no man who was his equal in either House of Congress. It was my good fortune to serve with him during three sessions of the 45th Congress, and I had good opportunities for comparing him with the most noted public men of the day. In largeness and breadth of culture, in clearness of discrimination, in accurate conception of principles and statement of facts, and in occasional and indeed not infrequent electric bursts of eloquence, he had neither peer nor rival. At times his magnificent periods would almost seem to shake the dome of the Capitol, approaching, if indeed he did not rival the Athenian orator when he "fulmined over Greece," and shook the throne of Philip.

In his personal bearing he was most winning, and more magnetic perhaps than any public man of our times, save Henry Clay. No man ever came within the circle of his personal influence and attraction, without being drawn to him "with cords of love and the bands of a man," and I may be pardoned for saying that it will ever be to me a proud and consoling reflection that even for a brief season I enjoyed his friendship and shared his confidence. Alas, that he was compelled to write, in the inexpressibly sad and perhaps prophetic words his failing hand and fainting heart were able to trace, "*Strangulatus pro Republica.*"

specific work was most fully and ably done by Dr. Fisher, in
the admirable jubilee discourse of 1862, to which I have already
alluded; and in the third place the doctrine of the "perseverance
of the saints," is not, I fear, so fully established in all your minds
as to enable your patience to hold out fairly to the end. I must
forego this task, and yet I may by your indulgence, perhaps, be
allowed to select from the honored list the first two and the last
two presidents for a brief and imperfect commemoration.

With regard to President Backus, it should perhaps be said his
fame was with me for the most part traditional, for I was too
young at the time of his accession to office to have a personal
acquaintance with him, and yet it was my good fortune as a boy
to listen to some three or four of those massive discourses by which
he attracted the attention not only, but roused, and kindled the
heart of Central New York. He was a man of large and rugged
frame, and his style of thought and expression was somewhat in
harmony with his physical presence. There might be applied to
him perhaps without much exaggeration the phrase by which the
Irish orator characterized the elder Pitt, "Original and unaccom-
modating, the features of his character had the hardihood of
antiquity." He never suppressed an opinion that he honestly
entertained for fear of awakening a prejudice, nor held back a
truth lest it might offend an esthetic taste. Truth was to him
"the immediate jewel of the soul," and he held it above all price
and subject to no politic accommodation. All this, however, was
but the outside shell, rough and rugged to the sight, but it inclosed
a heart as tender and sympathetic as a child. Masterly and
powerful as he was in discourse, his nature was strongly and deeply
emotional, and he rarely if ever closed the most energetic and
impressive sermon without in its final passages breaking out into
passionate appeals and tender implorations, and almost without
exception manifesting the depth of his emotion, and the yearning
strength of his love by a copious flow of tears.

In addition to these traits, it should be said of President Backus
that he was a man of quick apprehension and a keen sense of
humor, and I am inclined to think that the best part of the capital
of our college for wit is founded upon his lively sallies, his apt
retorts, and his cutting, although not ill-natured, sarcasms. They
are traditional in our college, and form a repertory upon which

the successive generations of students have been perpetually drawing for some of their best and brightest things.

President Davis came to our college as the successor of Backus with a high reputation both as a scholar and a preacher. This is clearly evidenced by the fact that he was simultaneously elected to the presidency of Yale and of Hamilton. He declined the former and accepted the latter, and held the office for the long term of sixteen years. He saw some stormy days, and passed through some trying scenes, but I truly believe that he was throughout most conscientious and sincere, and never doubted that he was acting in the line of duty. In manner he was most courteous and dignified, and always preserved a most even and equable temper. I ought to remember him, as I do with veneration not only, but with gratitude, for to my few merits he was very kind, to my manifold failures and errors he was very blind, or winked so hard that he either did not or affected not to see them, and so I got on smoothly and serenely over what otherwise might have been a somewhat rough and even tempestuous sea.

> "Peace to the memory of a man of worth,
> A man of letters and of manners, too."

Of the remaining list of presidents, until we reach the last two in the line, I propose, for the reasons I have already suggested, to make no remark but this, that while all the others preceding and following him save one, have gone to the land of silence, there yet remains with us of that goodly company one venerable form, the light of whose beneficent countenance and the benefit of whose large experience are still enjoyed by the Board of Trustees. Long may that light continue to shine, and that valued counsel be given. Of him I can say no better or worthier word than to repeat the felicitous quotation made by President Fisher from the Latin classic,

> " *Serus in cœlum redeas, diuque*
> *Lætus intersis nobis.*"

What I have now to say of the remaining two presidents, must be compressed into the briefest space. Of Dr. Fisher I had occasion to speak at some length in the commemorative discourse delivered soon after his lamented death, and I have no desire to change or qualify at all the estimate I then made of him as a man, a minister of the word, and as the presiding officer of our college. As a preacher he certainly stood in the front rank of American divines; he had a strong and steady purpose, and no small degree of executive ability. It may be that in matters of college discipline, he was a little too much of a martinet, and carried inquisition into minor offenses, involving no moral turpitude to an unwise extent, for although I may err in judgment in this regard, I still believe that in college government as in some other institutions, there are some things that may not either be seen, or if seen, be judiciously overlooked. But however this may have been, there can be no diversity of opinion in respect to the value and importance of the work accomplished by Dr. Fisher for the college outside its walls. In this enterprise he was untiring in labor and unflagging in zeal. He made the name of Hamilton widely known and honored, and a large debt of gratitude will ever be due to that man of blessed memory who gave himself to that most beneficent and most needful work.

Concerning the last in the line preceding him whom we this day induct into office, I realize distinctly the presence in which I speak, and that will prevent me from saying much that my heart would prompt and my voice willingly utter. But even that presence will not restrain me from declaring my unqualified conviction that in high and finished culture, in purity of purpose and conscientious discharge of duty, in harmonious relationship with those more immediately associated with him in the college government; above all in the courteous demeanor of the true gentleman, and the entire self-control and the Christ-like spirit exhibited by him in scenes of more than common trial and difficulty, he was not excelled, if indeed he was equalled by any of his predecessors.

If now there shall be united in harmonious combination in the coming man, the varied gifts and distinguishing characteristics of these two illustrious and immediate forerunners, the outcome will be that perfect president we all have been looking for, and whom we now hail as the new incumbent of this exalted trust.

President Darling, a high and noble work is before you. An enlarged, a liberal, a Christian education is not a new thing in the history of our college, nor is it now for the first time to be inaugurated here. The foundations of this institution were laid by the faithful missionary Kirkland, and his inspiration was the oft-repeated prayer that its establishment might "under the smiles of the God of wisdom prove an eminent means of diffusing useful knowledge. enlarging the bounds of human happiness, and aiding the reign of virtue and the kingdom of the blessed Redeemer."

These great ends have never been lost sight of in all the nearly seventy years of our history. Most emphatically was the last great lesson emphasized by President Fisher in his inaugural discourse, and faithfully has it been carried out by his successor in office. May yours be the happy mission of following these illustrious precedents, and yours the high privilege in the coming years to send forth from this seat of science, learning and religion. bands of cultivated and ingenuous youth who in their daily lives shall illustrate and exemplify the lessons they shall here have learned. by exhibiting the full and matured fruits of a ripe scholarship, a highly cultured intellect. a noble manliness. a warm Christian heart, and an earnest and active Christian faith.

Representing, as I do, the Board of Trustees. I hesitate not to pledge to you their full and hearty support in every well-directed effort to enlarge the influence and enhance the reputation of our college, and as their organ I now place in your hands the Charter, the Key and the Seal of this Institution. They constitute your investiture and are the insignia of your authority and power. The Charter is the fundamental law which governs us all; the Key in an emblematic sense is to be employed in opening that temple of knowledge and wisdom into which you are to invite and conduct its youthful votaries, and with the Seal you are to impress upon mind and soul imperishable lessons and undying records.

May all that we hope and you anticipate be fully and success. fully achieved, and may you receive, in the discharge of your high functions, the abundant and approving smile of that "God of wisdom," whose presence and power the sainted Kirkland so ardently invoked.

ACCEPTING THE INSIGNIA OF OFFICE.

AT the conclusion of Judge Bacon's address, after receiving the Charter. Seal and Keys of the College, President Darling addressing the speaker, trustees and faculty, said that he accepted with diffidence and distrust from the representative of the Board of Trustees, the insignia of his office as President of Hamilton

College. He realized as clearly as any one that the presidency of a college like Hamilton is no sinecure. He had been emboldened to assume the task by the urgent wishes and earnest encouragement of life-long friends and with the hope that it was the will of the Master. He had no promises to make on entering upon his duties, but pledged his best efforts and energies to the sacred trust that had been imposed upon him. He had heard with pleasure the well deserved and kindly references to his distinguished predecessor, President BROWN, and felicitated himself that his future home would not be so far distant from College Hill that he could not often avail himself of the valuable advice that his successful experience had so well fitted him to give.

This was followed by President Darling's Inaugural Discourse. When Dr. Darling had finished his discourse, the students sang a

HYMN OF WELCOME.

Tune—PARK STREET.

I.

With grace to choose the Bible's creed,
And follow it in word and deed,
Straight on thro' good report and ill,
God bless our Mother on the Hill.

II.

To be a shield when armies fail,
A beacon light when storms assail,
Thro' days of darkness hoping still,
God help our Mother on the Hill.

III.

With sons devout, in battle brave
To serve the Church, our land to save,
With ranks that wait their Leader's will,
God bless our Mother on the Hill.

IV.

Then welcome friends with helping hands,
And welcome lore from distant lands;
Thrice welcome Leader, toil and drill,
With Blessed Mother on the Hill.

ADDRESS OF THE REV. DR. UPSON.

The Rev. Dr. Anson J. Upson, and the Rev. Dr. Irenaeus Prime made addresses of fellowship. Dr. Upson said:

4

President Darling:

It is with sincere pleasure that I am permitted at this time to address words of fellowship and congratulation to you.

During the past ten years our personal relations have been increasingly intimate. We have been Christian ministers in the same capital city. We have labored together as pastors of neighboring and affiliated churches. We have been bound together as members of the same ministerial brotherhood. We have often conversed together of things pertaining to the kingdom of God. We have often heartily united in many plans for the promotion of the kingdom of our common Lord. And now you have come into this new sphere of duty closely allied to my own. You have come under the influence of associations here that are not only hallowed in my memory, but which have blessed the larger portion of my life. Permit me most sincerely to congratulate the college and yourself. And let me frankly say that I do this because, with some knowledge of the peculiar responsibilities of the place into which, as I believe, God, in his providence, has called you, I recognize also your peculiar fitness for this difficult and responsible and influential position.

Let me say, too, that I am not alone in the conviction, that by your scholarship, by your industry, by your energy, by your executive force, by your practical wisdom, for which Cicero has given us a single word—by your *prudentia*, in the past, you have already given abundant assurance of success in the immediate future.

Many of us, Mr. President, are familiar with your habits of exhaustive study. We recognize your self-controlled enthusiasm in the best things. Many of us appreciate your wisdom already shown in the development of youthful character and influence, and in the control and direction of powerful churches. We know how wise and strong you have been as a leader of men, upon the platform, and in the guidance of a great assembly. To those of us who are thus familiar with your career these characteristics are a presage of increasing influence and success in your new position. With such convictions as these, I need hardly repeat, it is for myself a real pleasure to recognize our fellowship, and to speak words of congratulation to you to-day.

And yet I do not for a moment suppose, that merely because of our personal relations, or because of any peculiar fitness in myself,

1. THE REV. DR. EDWARD ROBINSON, '16.
2. HON. GERRIT SMITH, '18.
3. GEN'L JOHN KNOX, (TRUSTEE).
4. PROF. CHAS. AVERY, '20.
5. PROF. OREN ROOT, '33.
6. PROF. EDWARD NORTH, '41.
7. PROF. C. H. F. PETERS.
8. PROF. A. J. UPSON, '43.

I have been called to address you now. Others are here who have long been identified with the history of this college, and who honor this occasion by their presence, who could speak to you with far greater impressiveness and eloquence.

THE COLLEGE AND THE REGENTS.

And yet, providentially, I have been so placed, in such relations, that I am enabled to convey to you congratulations much more significant than any merely personal words can express. The Regents of the University of the State of New York, who have the supervision of the colleges and academies of the State, have always cherished sentiments of peculiar esteem and regard for Hamilton College. Permit me, Mr. President, as a member of the board, to express to you and your associates, our heartiest congratulations and good wishes. The college received its charter from the Board of Regents nearly seventy years ago. In age you are the third college in the State. The distinguished statesman after whom your college is named, and who was one of its early patrons, was the author of the statute which organized the Board of Regents. Five members of the board are graduates of this college. Its efficient secretary and assistant secretary, for many years, are among your most honored graduates. The learning and influence of your officers of instruction and government, have often been recognized in the convocations that have been held in Albany under the auspices of the board. No educational papers there have been read of greater interest and value than those contributed from this college. And no college in New York has been more loyal to the educational interests of our own commonwealth, than has the college which bears the name of the great political genius of the State and the Union, Alexander Hamilton.

We have no doubt that the traditions of the college in this regard will be perpetuated by yourself. It is the earnest desire and present purpose of the Board of Regents to make their influence increasingly felt in the higher education of New York, and to stimulate in every legitimate way the collegiate as well as the academical education of the State, so that the sons of New York need no longer neglect their own, so that the sons of New York need no longer cross the borders of their own commonwealth, to gain what they conceive to be the highest educational advantages.

With these plans, we believe, that you, sir, and your associates will sympathize. And in this belief the Regents of the University of New York congratulate themselves, as well as you to-day.

HAMILTON, AUBURN SEMINARY AND THE CHURCH.

And you will not be surprised, sir, that as a Professor in Auburn Theological Seminary, I bring you the fraternal greetings of its authorities, and of all our theological seminaries. You are an alumnus of Auburn Theological Seminary, and the first alumnus of that institution who has been elected president of this college. We feel ourselves honored by your election to this influential position. The natural union of the seminary and the college is thus, we believe, recognized and emphasized. For the two are essentially one. We have a similiar history ; we have largely the same friends ; we have a common constituency, a common patronage and a similar purpose. Less than a hundred miles apart, railways and telegraphs and telephones are rapidly enabling us to live within hearing, if not in sight, of each other.

Of the 1,230 ministers who have pursued their studies in Auburn Theological Seminary, 277 were graduates or undergraduates of Hamilton College—a number large enough to indicate that we are very closely related and reciprocally interested in each other's prosperity. We would not be divorced, and you will not divorce us. Of the 1,230 ministers who have pursued their professional studies in Auburn Seminary, 999 have been college-bred men. We believe in college-bred ministers, and so do you ; and therefore we can not fail to be greatly interested in each other's work.

We bid you and your associates, Mr. President, Godspeed in all your efforts to add to the resources of this college, and to perpetuate and increase the thoroughness and breadth of its scholarship. No talents can be too great, no learning can be too profound, no culture can be too thorough to consecrate to Christ and His church.

And let me, in the name of the Christian ministers and churches of the State, welcome you to this position into which God has called you. This is a college founded by a Christian missionary, for the advancement of " the kingdom of the blessed Redeemer "—the " light " of the gospel has illuminated its halls—the " truth " of the gospel has been taught by its instructors. Of its 2,200 graduates, 625 have been Christian ministers. May it ever be a Christian college. Palsied be the tongue that, in yonder chairs of instruction, shall ever deny the truth as it is in Jesus!

The Christian people of this State, sir, welcome you to your high place, as a representative Christian minister. For they are thus assured that the truth here taught will be expressed in words that have no uncertain sound.

And more than this: Most of us are thoroughly convinced that a Christian college must look largely for its support and patronage to some particular Christian denomination, to which it stands in a kind of representative relation. We believe "it is a strong guaranty of the permanence and success of a college to be entrenched in the affections and sympathies of a Christian people, who feel a special responsibility as to its fortunes, and a special joy and pride in its fame and influence." Sectarian peculiarities should not be offensively obtruded; a narrow, proselyting spirit should be condemned; conscientious convictions should not be rudely assailed in the public and official instructions given; and yet the influence of the college in this direction should not be indefinite and negative, but pronounced and positive. The religious tone of the institution should be clearly defined, so that patrons may know the kind of influence that in this respect will surround their sons; so that donors may be sure their gifts will not be diverted. In that most intelligent commonwealth on our eastern border, large sums that have been given in the past to "Christ and the church," are in danger to-day of being transferred to the agnostics. By pursuing a policy of uncertainty or indifference in this direction, a college gains nothing, and loses much.

Do not misunderstand me; a college will not depend, for its prosperity, exclusively upon the religious sympathy of its patrons and friends. By no means. A college will also depend largely for its prosperity upon its location, upon its scholarship, upon its reputation for good learning and thorough instruction, upon its libraries and other appliances for education, upon the good will of its alumni, upon the sympathy and affection that will gather round it in the progress of years.

And yet, prominent among these sources of prosperity, perhaps leading them all, are those conscientious convictions that bind to it patrons and friends with hooks of steel. For a Christian college to disregard altogether this source of life and power, is suicide!

Because we believe that you, sir, sympathize with these views, the Presbyterian ministers and churches of this State greet you to-day. You believe as we do, that the relation between the Presbyterian Church and this college is reciprocal, and should be close and permanent. The church needs the college, and the college needs the church.

Both propositions are true—one is as true as the other. Why not have a Nassau Hall? Why not have a Princeton College in New York, as well as in New Jersey? Your location is similar. The organization of the University of the State, under the supervision of the Regents, pre-supposes that each of the colleges shall represent some phase of religious opinion. Why not concentrate here the same abundant wealth and learning and culture that have made the College of New Jersey increasingly renowned all over the earth? Why not gather here a similar reservoir of Christian influence, that shall fertilize the world?

THE COLLEGE AND THE ALUMNI.

But, Mr. President, as one of the graduates of this college, I am also permitted to represent the alumni, and greet you with cordiality as our leader.

As graduates of Hamilton College, we, sir, consider ourselves to be a very respectable body. More than two thousand two hundred men have marched in our ranks, and to-day our little army among the living is seventeen hundred strong. Some of us have stood before kings. Many of us, we think, have been useful to the State as executive officers and law-makers. Some of us upon the bench, we believe, have faithfully administered justice and enforced the laws. We know that others of our number have become deservedly trusted financiers; and others still have wielded a wide influence in the marts of trade. Many have healed the sick, and many more, in this land or in foreign countries, have cared for the souls of men.

On the roll of our army are the names of many scholars and teachers, and some distinguished authors. We have certainly made our voices heard from the pulpit and from the platform, at the bar and in the senate.

1. EMMONS CLARK   47, COL. 7ᵀᴴ REG., N. Y.
3. U. S. SENATOR HENRY B. PAYNE, '42.
5. HON. ELIHU ROOT, '64.
7. PROF. EDWARD F. B. ORTON, '48.

U. B. SENAT. D'EAN   PRATT, '51
4. CHAS. DUDLEY WARNER, '51
6. U. S. SENAT. H. B. H. HARRIS, '47
8. HON. THEO. W. DWIGHT, '42.

To be sure, not many years ago, in the city of New York, there was a closely contested competition by under-graduates in the department of public speech, in which very many of the leading colleges of the country took part. To be sure, in advertising the competition, they did placard, all over the city, the name of our little college at the very end of the list of colleges, in very small letters, entitling us "and Hamilton." We could find no fault with the arrangement or the style. It was very natural.

Neither could we blame our enthusiastic boys if, at the end of the competition, when the victory was gained by one of their number, they did—taking him on their shoulders and carrying him out of the hall—shout till the welkin rang, somewhat in derision, the no longer humiliating words, "and Hamilton."

But we would not make too much of trifles. We would not be too sensitive. We are among the smaller colleges. And yet every one may have wondered why our remarkable merit has not been recognized invariably by the authorities of our own college. Some may have wondered why some graduate has not been made president! There is no mystery about it. Hamilton graduates are all otherwise engaged. The business in which they are employed is too important to be left!

Besides, they know by experience that their own little college does not need their help. It is attractive enough to draw to itself the very best in the land. Have we not drawn five of our presidents from one of the two largest colleges in the country? And did not the second of these five deliberately prefer to succeed Azel Backus here rather than Timothy Dwight at New Haven? Did it not require the combined power of both the universities of Dublin and Glasgow to educate for us our fourth president! And have we not attracted another, one of her most cultured sons from the halls of Dartmouth? And now we have to thank Amherst College for another leader. And in truth, we are grateful. With no affectation we can seriously say, that with all our own ability and learning, these imported instructors have done us good. They have given us ideas which, perhaps, we ourselves might never have originated. They have introduced new methods of education which the experience of other colleges has proved to be useful. While correcting our faults, they have not been blind to our merits.

Mr. President, our salutations are fraternal. It is a cheering indication of the increasing heartiness of our people, that more than our fathers, we are recognizing our college relations and expressing our attachment. Graduates are gathering in larger numbers every year, to celebrate college anniversaries. The alumni of Hamilton College share this spirit of the times, in their desire to express in every possible way their enthusiastic attachment to their educational home. We want to be enthusiastic. We do not want to be ashamed of our enthusiasm. We are glad to have more and more substantial reasons for it, in the ability, the learning and the accurate scholarship of yourself and your associates. We want to have more and more substantial reasons for it, in the surpassing excellence of the education here given.

The graduates of this college are not rich. So far as I know there are not many millionaires among us. If there be the benevolent eyes of our financial commissioner—our college procurator will soon discover them! The graduates of Hamilton College are not rich. But we are wealthy in the treasures of our good-will and affection for this venerable college. We love our mother on the hill. We can never forget what she has done for us. God bless her!

And, Mr. President, these, my old friends and neighbors, among whom I have lived so long, will not think me presumptuous if I say to you, for them, that you will not long be a stranger in this beautiful valley. Your experience will be very different from my own, if you do not receive a cordial welcome to their hearts, their homes and their churches. You will never know, in this world, some of the best of these. God has taken them. I wish you could have know them as I did. How such men as Judge Williams and Dr. Gridley would have encouraged your heart and strengthened your hands! But their helpful influence remains. It has entered largely into the formation of the character of this community, and will not pass away.

Not only in this immediate vicinity, but in the city near us, and throughout Central New York, the influence of the college is felt and recognized. It has educated many who might not otherwise have received a collegiate education. The obligation is largely felt. It is acknowledged. It can be appealed to successfully.

I have thus endeavored to express to you, Mr. President, the cordial greeting of those who are sincerely interested in the prosperity of this seat of learning. I may not have echoed the sentiments of every one. But whatever infelicities may have characterized what has been said, however we may have failed to express the convictions of all, one thing, I hope, is evident—that for myself and those I represent, we belong to neither of two classes: We have no sympathy with one class who have no faith in the college, nor with another class who expect too much of it.

There are those who have but little or no faith in this college. If it lives, if it drags out a half lifeless existence, it far surpasses their expectations. And, therefore, they are content with any facilities or with any results. They wonder how anybody can give anything to such a hopeless enterprise. They wonder how anybody can accept a place among its officers of instruction or government. If they give anything to it themselves, or send any one here to be educated, it is under compulsion. They have no faith in it.

And, on the other hand, there are those who expect too much. Great numbers should throng its halls. Its course of study should be enlarged into the curriculum of a university. They compare it with institutions four times as old, and wonder why this stripling has not the vigor and the power of mature manhood. They remember that dear, precious old myth, about Minerva springing full-armed from the brain of Jupiter, a myth that they have heard repeated every commencement since their childhood, and somehow they expect the college will realize it. In their desire to accomplish so much they do not appreciate what has already been done.

COLLEGE IMPROVEMENTS.

Now I need not say that for myself and those I represent, we do not sympathize with either of these two classes. I preach to-day no doctrine of despair. We have faith in the college because of what has already been done, and we would have reasonable expectations only for the future. We would obey the exhortation of the psalmist and not "forget all His benefits." We would not murmur so much over what we have not as to forget what we have. Mr. President, you have doubtless already discovered that many improvements are here needed, and many enlargements may here be made. But I think you would be greatly encouraged in your good work if, in your mind's eye, you could carry, as I do, the picture of yonder college as I saw it in 1840, in my boyhood, when my name was first enrolled in one of its classes. Why, sir, the cold, bare and dingy room into which I was introduced was enough to depress the exuberant spirits of the most irrepressible sophomore. There is no such room there now. I had left a pleasant home in the city of Utica, and the first thing they asked me when I entered the room was whether I had brought my mantel piece.

In those days rough brick jambs were thought to be good enough for college boys. They don't think so now. But I had to buy a wooden mantel piece, and I tied it to the chimney with nails and strings.

In those days the north end of the college campus was a desert, stript of all its verdure. There were no flowers. There was no observatory then. Our "royal Dane," our glorious cannoneer, was not then "assaulting the skies" with his artillery.

North college, Dexter Hall, had been half finished, but the students were chopping up the inside for kindling wood. The college chapel, in its artistic proportions one of the most graceful buildings in the State, was in the inside just as rough and marred and sculptured as such rooms used to be, but are not now. To find the library, I climbed up into the third story of the chapel, where the little collection of books was mixed up with geological and mineralogical specimens. Genesis and geology, if not reconciled, were in close proximity there.

The chemical laboratory was down in the cellar of the chapel. Our venerable friend, Professor Avery, then in the maturity of his powers, was doing his best down there to analyze light, in the midst of darkness. The now convenient laboratory was unbuilt.

In the spacious hall where now are gathered Prof. Root's invaluable collections was a carpenter's shop. The south college was not half covered with crumbling stucco. The little college campus was enclosed with a wooden fence and guarded all around by a row of ancient poplars. Now, without question, on yonder hillside is the most beautiful college campus in all the land, and I have seen the most of them. No college in the State has a better library building. These and the other facilities I have named, are the accumulations of a single generation.

If you, Mr. President, could see this college as I saw it in 1840,

SENIOR HILL.
JUNIOR HILL.
SOPHOMORE HILL.

PROF. BRANDT'S.

VIEW ON CAMPUS.

GENERAL MASS HOUSE TO THE LINE.

and contrast it with what you see there to-day, it would strengthen your faith.

And when I remember how God has blessed this college with men of such ability and scholarship to preside over it, two of whom are living and honored here to-day; when I remember how, in spite of all the evident disadvantages of this position, faithful instructors have here given the best of their life to the education of hundreds of young men, and when, as I read your triennial catalogue, there rise before me so many living forms with their bright and beautiful faces, some of whom have gone down in the smoke of battle, and most of whom are blessing the world by their labors for God and man ; when I remember the many occasions where the influences of the Holy Spirit have been especially felt by the young men gathered in those old halls : and the many times when great numbers have there been " renewed in the temper and spirit of their minds," and made "heirs of God and joint heirs with Christ ; " when I think of all these, I will not believe that God will let this College die! If I may say so, too much has been invested here for God to permit it to be lost.

You have come here, sir, at a propitious time. The blessings of God have been recently poured upon this nation : the avenues of trade are crowded with business. Commerce with foreign nations was never so prosperous. Streams of gold have been flowing into the coffers of the nation, till there is not room to contain them.

You have come at a propitious time to be president of this Christian college. The assassination of our chief magistrate has brought out the latent Christian faith of this people as never before.

We do believe in prayer. We worship the God of our fathers. We are a Christian people, and we mean to sustain and develop Christian institutions. With one heart and mind we repeat the beautiful hymn of one of your own associates, suggested by the motto on your college seal, " *Lux et Veritas :* "

> Welcome, thou servant of the Lord !
>   Lift high the quenchless torch of truth ;
> With purest light from God's own word,
>   Guide thou the steps of generous youth.
>
> Be thine the high and holy part,
>   Lessons to teach that heavenward lead ;
> And thine the hungry mind and heart
>   With daily bread of life to feed.

Allies unseen thy steps attend,
And saints redeemed thy service share;
Upward from many a Christian friend
Ascends for thee the strength of prayer.

THE REV. DR. PRIME'S ADDRESS.

Mr. President and Gentlemen of the Board of Trustees:

The college. the church and the country are to be congratulated on the event that marks this day and makes it memorable. A city set on a hill can not be hid, and a college with such a history as Hamilton has, with its long line of illustrious presidents and professors. and a host of alumni adorning the Church and the State, must become a glory in the land, when it reflects the added luster of such a burning and shining light as this day appears in the firmament of learning.

As a trustee of two sister colleges I bring the hearty good wishes of both, and of all colleges that stand by the oracles of eternal truth and teach only what they *know*. In this day of conflict between truth and error, between knowledge and science, it is a cause for profound congratulation that this institution has installed in its presidential chair, a gentleman of honored lineage, a Chris-.ian scholar, a stalwart divine, a man of large and liberal views, of strong common sense, with knowledge of men and letters, who will give high tone to the work of education, while he illustrates in his person and his life the dignity and benediction of sound. manly. religious learning. I have long known him in the councils of the church of which he is one of the leaders, and of whose general assembly he is now the moderator. Among the five thousand ministers serving at her altars, not one is more admirably fitted to sustain. exalt and perpetuate the reputation of Hamilton College.

Supported by a faculty whose fame is identified with the stars, he will make this college, (bright as the past has been,) to shine more and more unto the perfect day.

The retiring president, Dr. Brown, rests on the well-earned rewards of a faithful, successful and honored administration. He carries with him the respect, affection and best wishes of the friends of Hamilton college. God grant that he and his beloved family may rejoice in his prolonged and increasing usefulness, till they rest from labor in the joy of the Lord.

Mr. President, a few days in this valley of wondrous wealth and beauty, have revealed to me its admirable fitness as the site of a college of the first rank among American schools of learning. The principles and spirit of your inaugural address to which we have just listened with profound gratification, inspire the assurance that such must be the rank of an institution over which you preside. The valley of the Mohawk, unexcelled in fertility and prosperity, teeming with richness and intelligence, its thousand church spires drawing down the blessings of heaven, ought to complete the endowment of this college without a year's delay.

Rejoicing with you in the circumstances of cheer and hope under which you enter upon your high calling, and invoking the enthusiastic rally of the alumni, and the favor of Him whose knowledge is light and life, I pray that this day may be one which you, Mr. President and the college, will remember always with gratitude and pleasure.

The Benediction was pronounced by the Rev. Dr. L. Merrill Miller, of Ogdensburg.

MINISTERS OF THE GOSPEL.

Since his inauguration President Darling has made earnest efforts to increase the endowment of Hamilton and widen its usefulness. It especially behooves the Presbyterian Church, always deservedly regarded the staunch friend of Christian learning, to heed the loud calls of the Institution for larger endowments, because such numbers of Hamilton graduates are entering the ministry. In the Synod of New York, 1888, were fifty-nine Yale, fifty-eight Williams, fifty-five Amherst, eighty-six Princeton, and one hundred and thirty-eight Hamilton men. At the New York City Hamilton alumni dinner, in 1887, it was said that Hamilton furnished more men for the ministry than Yale. A large percentage of Auburn Theological students came from Clinton. Union Theological Seminary, which has enjoyed the invaluable services of Hamilton's eminent alumnus, Dr. Edward Robinson, and two of whose Presidents, Rev. Dr. Joel Parker and Rev. Dr. Thomas S. Hastings graduated at Hamilton, always has a large representation from the College on its rolls. Hamilton names are also found in the catalogues of other "Schools of the Prophets," both among professors and students. If the church will do as much for the old institution at Clinton as the institution has done for the church, the college will soon receive an abundance of "the yellow dust which men call gold," to convert into sanctified learning.

COLLEGE PROFESSORS.

Hamilton has been fortunate in having among its professors such scholars and teachers as Dr. Josiah Noyes, Dr. James Hadley, Prof. Seth Norton, Dr. Theo. Strong, Dr. John Wayland, brother of President Wayland, of Brown University, Dr. Charles Avery, Prof. Marcus Catlin, Dr. T. W. Dwight, Dr. Henry Mandeville, Dr. Anson J. Upson, the Rev. Wm. N. McHarg, Dr. Ellicott Evans, and Dr. Oren Root, who gathered during his professorship the splendid collection of minerals and geological specimens which now form the "Root Collection" in Knox Hall. His son, Edward Walstein Root, was for a brief period Child's Professor of Agricultural Chemistry, but in the prime of his manhood and usefulness he was stricken, and his promising life brought to a close. Other members of the Faculty, Hamilton Alumni will remember with gratitude. Among them, The Rev. Dr. N. W. Goertner, the kind-hearted College Pastor, and the successful Commissioner, who in his appeals for funds once said : "There is none so poor that he is not able to do something. If he cannot bring a wreath with which to crown the head of the good old mother, let him at least pluck a single flower and place it on her brow or lay it on her bosom, accompanied with the earnest prayer that God's blessing may continue to rest upon her." Those who were privileged to enjoy the instruction of another faithful Professor, the Rev. Dr. John W. Mears, will never forget his love of letters and of the state.

Professors A. P. Kelsey, Oren Root, Jr., A. G. Hopkins, H. C. G. Brandt, Arthur S. Hoyt, Anthony H. Evans, and Clinton Scollard of the present Faculty are Hamilton men. Upon the last has fallen the mantle of song. He is one of the American poets, who is helping to make the land "a nest of singing birds." Dr. A. H. Chester is a graduate of Union and Columbia, and Dr. Edward J. Hamilton, of Hanover College.

EDWARD NORTH, L. H. D., LL. D.

"The Hamiltonian" for 1888, published a brief biographical sketch of Professor Edward North, L. H. D., LL. D., a nephew of

1. PROF. E. J. HAMILTON, (HANOVER)
3. PROF. OREN ROOT, JR., '56.
5. PROF. A. G. HOPKINS, '66.
7. PROF. A. B. HOYT, '72.
9. ASS'T PROF. A. H. EVANS, '82.

Ex-President North. As student, professor, and trustee he has been identified with the college fifty years. To his hillside home, known as the thoughts of many graduates gratefully go.

The biographer writes.

"We are sure that the present number of 'The Hamiltonian' will come with a special pleasure to every alumnus of Hamilton because of the excellent likeness which we present of Professor Edward North. Several years ago when that gifted and brilliant lecturer, Mr. William Parsons, delivered to a Clinton audience his lecture upon 'Homer,' after being introduced by Professor North, he at once began: "In bringing this old Greek before you"—when he was interrupted by a storm of applause. The puzzled lecturer could hardly understand that to the sons of Hamilton his opening words did not suggest

'The blind old bard of Scio's rocky isle.'

but a more modern poet, teacher and man of letters. And so we believe that the "boys," gray-haired as well as young, scattered all over our state and country, will dispense with all titles of dignity as they look upon this face, and exclaim with words, not of irreverence, but of affection: "there's old Greek!" Men immersed in business cares, and whose heads are sprinkled with silver, will fancy that they sit once more upon the old pine benches of twenty years ago, and try to catch the music of Homer's verse. They will catch once again the echoes of a voice once so familiar in the class-room, as it summoned them with its lingering but musical monotone to render an Idyl of Theocritus or a strophe of Greek tragedy. They will listen once more to the lecture on the old Greek Lexicon, and vow that the dog-eared and thumb-stained volume shall be their companion through life.

Professor North's professional career covers considerably more than half of the period of the entire life of the College. He has served under four presidents—Drs. North, Fisher, Brown and Darling—and his recollection as a student goes back to the time of Dr. Penney, who was fourth in office from Dr. Backus. He has held office for a period longer by ten years than any other officer who has ever been connected with this College. He has been identified, therefore, with all that is best in her history.

with the period of her greatest growth and expansion. He knows
her history and embodies her traditions and spirit more thoroughly
than any other alumnus of Hamilton. He has known, and lived
and labored with some of the self-sacrificing men who stood by
the cradle of our alma mater. The campus has been beautified,
new buildings have been added, the course of instruction has been
enlarged and modified, the constitution of the corps of instructors
has been entirely changed ; while Professor North, though still in
the vigor of life, remains, connecting the present with the past, and
giving a sort of permanence and continuity to the college history.
When Louis XIV. said ' *L'etat, c'est moi,*' he expressed something
more than a mere feeling of conceit and arrogance. In a good
sense he might have meant, " I embody the spirit, I feel the pulse,
I think the thoughts of my people; the life of the state flows
through my veins ; my heart beats in tune with the popular
heart." In a humbler way may it be said that Professor North
represents the college. He is the most prominent figure in the
foreground. His life has long run parallel with her life. She has
no more steadfast friend and servant. She has no better expo-
nent of her culture. The alumnus who thinks of the college thinks
first of him. These two pictures—the school of learning and the
loyal instructor—are seldom separated in the consciousness of the
graduates of Hamilton.

When Professor North entered upon his work the Faculty was
constituted as follows: President, Simeon North ; Professor of
Chemistry, Charles Avery ; Mathematics, Marcus Catlin ; Rhetoric and Moral Philosophy, Henry Mandeville; Tutor, Theodore
W. Dwight. To this list of distinguished names that of Edward
North was added, as Professor of Greek and Latin. This was in
the year 1843. So that in June, 1888, he will have completed
the forty-fifth year of his service. Other instructors have held
office for long periods, and have come in contact with hundreds
of young men, but in these respects Professor North's career is
unique.

A COMPARATIVE STATEMENT.

A comparative statement may be interesting, showing the term
of office of various instructors and the number of students who
received diplomas while they were in office:

Name.	Length of Service.	No. of Students.
Charles Avery,	35 years,	969
Oren Root,	35 "	1,058
Simeon North,	28 "	639
Anson J. Upson	25 "	806
Marcus Catlin,	15 "	372
Samuel G. Brown,	15 "	494
Ellicott Evans,	22 "	731
Edward North,	45 "	1,450

The entire body of living alumni numbers about 2,600. It is evident, therefore, that considerably more than half of this num-number have received instruction at the hands of Professor North. Probably two-thirds of the students graduated in the classical course have thus come in contact with him, since the aggregate number given above includes also the graduates of the law school.

Professor North's services to the College have been inestimable and varied. His work as an instructor has had a pronounced and permanent value; yet this is but one of the many lines of activity in which he has done good service to the College, to its graduates and to the general cause of education. In public addresses, in contact with schools and teachers throughout the State, in the work of the convocation at Albany, his influence has been quietly but deeply felt. He has often been the unknown power to whose influence or advice were due many of the movements in the academic world. A quasi power of appointment to many of our New York schools has for many years resided in his hands, and the long and successful line of instructors in Robert College, Constantinople, found its origin, and in many cases its continuance, in consultations with him. A more subtle influence, contributing positively to the strength of the College, has been found in Professor North's constant and varied correspondence with our alumni. The stroke of his pen has started a throb of interest in the almost fossil heart of many an alumnus beginning to be oblivious of his alma mater. Through the medium of these numberless letters, the tide of sympathy and affection has been kept moving to and fro between the College and her widely-scattered sons. Not merely in the line of sentiment has this labor been of value. It has furnished us statistics of a most interesting sort.

5

It has kept us informed as to all matters of importance in connection with the lives and labors of our alumni. The contributions under the head of 'Necrology' and 'Alumniana,' in the "Hamilton Literary Monthly," have cost much time and labor; and, though often overlooked by those in search of 'literature,' will be found hereafter to have a positive and permanent value.

Professor North's skill and success as an instructor have been founded upon his painstaking fidelity, his untiring patience and his inexhaustible sympathy with young men, even with the dull and indolent. Dr. Arnold once blazed out in wrath upon a pupil who was making bad work of a passage in Greek, but was silenced at once by the reply: 'I am doing as well as I can, sir.' Our modern interpreter of Thucydides is not provoked, even by dullness, to the language of satire or anger. The patience which assisted the feebly equipped student of thirty years ago over the perplexing archaisms of Homer, or through the bewildering forms of the dialect of Theocritus, is still unexhausted and still finds ample room for exercise. '*The poor*,' said Dr. Upson with reference to scholarship and not to property, '*the poor ye have ever with you*;' and such poverty has ever found abundant sympathy and help in the incumbent of the Greek chair. But above and beyond all this there is another fact which may serve to explain the success and the charm which have attended upon the instruction of Professor North. There is a subtle power, it is said, in every foreign language, which eludes and defies an attempt to transfer a master-piece from such a language to our own. It is at least true that it requires a poet to translate a poet. In Professor North the power of imagination and of poetic, expression is highly developed. His style of composition in prose has an indefinable element of music and rhythm. Though often using polysyllabic words, his language is certainly melodious. His ventures in song have given proof of a power to array thought in a graceful and poetic garb.

His power of expressing truth in striking and epigrammatic forms is rare, and is witnessed in the list of class mottoes running through more than a quarter of a century. These mottoes, if collected, would form a series of maxims, inspiring and practical, equal almost to those of Cato or of Benjamin Franklin. They illustrate a power of felicitous expression, in Greek as well as in English, which few men possess. This happy faculty appears in

the class-room interpretation of the Greek poets. The flavor of
the original is not lost in the English version. The musical
Greek is also musical English. The Greek compound, which, in
the hands of a novice, contains nothing but a crude jargon,
becomes, in the hands of the master, smooth and melodious. The
poetic rendering, the happy collocation of words, the apt phrase,
the coinage even of new expressions to meet the demands of the
original, are all familiar to those who have studied under Dr.
North. He is permeated with the spirit of Greek life and letters,
and his style of thought and composition is quite as much Attic as
English. But we must leave memory to do the rest of the work
and to add the finishing touches to this very adequate and frag-
mentary sketch. These few words will serve to start lines of
thought which will call up in many minds pleasant recollections
of the past. May the sons of Hamilton long find it their privilege to study the masterpieces of Greek literature under the
guidance of a scholar so genial and so wise as Dr. Edward
North."

New York alumni, who were at the Astor House re-union years
ago, will not soon forget Dr. North's poem on Hamilton College—the poem closing with these lines:

"All hail to the Dame whose voice on the Hill,
Wakes her sons to survey thought's kingdom at will;
And arms them to wield in their glad golden youth,
Ithuriel's spear and the falchion of truth.
Then crown Alma Mater with honors forever·
Let her plenty and peace flow deep like a river;
Let her names be all sweet, Homeric and tender,
Bright-throned, silver-footed, fair Learning's Defender."

DR. C. H. F. PETERS.

"The Hamiltonian" recently gladdened many graduates by
placing before them the pictured-face of Dr. C. H. F. Peters,
Director of the Litchfield Observatory, and Professor of Astronomy
in Hamilton College more than thirty years. The great Astron-
omer has indeed written his own name and that of the College
among the stars. Forty-seven of the asteroids were discovered
by him. Only scholars can appreciate the prodigious work he has
done in preparing his "star charts" which include thousands of
stars. In 1874 he was placed by the U. S. Government in charge
of the party which in the U. S. Gunboat Swatara, went to New

Zealand to observe the transit of Venus. The observations were very successful and complete. The King of Sweden has presented Dr. Peters with a gold metal for his discoveries concerning the sun, and recently he also received the Cross of the French Legion of Honor.

"The Hamiltonian," 1889, also gratified students and alumni by publishing a biographical sketch of

ALBERT HUNTINGTON CHESTER, E. M. PH.D.,

the fifth Professor of Chemistry in Hamilton College. Dr. Albert Huntington Chester, was born November 22d, 1843, in Saratoga Springs, N. Y., where his father, Rev. Dr. A. T. Chester, was then pastor of the First Presbyterian Church. After two years in Union College, he entered the School of Mines in New York City, and was a member of the second class that was graduated from that department of Columbia College. The high distinction he had won as a student under Professors Egleston, Chandler and Newberry in the School of Mines, opened the way for his election in 1870, to succeed Professor E. W. Root. He at once removed to Clinton, and for eighteen years has discharged the duties of his professorship with fidelity, enthusiasm and the largest success. His routine of class work includes instruction and lectures in general Chemistry, in Analytical, Agricultural and Medical Chemistry, and in Mineralogy. The privileges of the laboratory are also open to graduates and special students, who are furnished with excellent facilities for chemical investigations, including the analysis of ores and technical products.

Professor Chester's conscientious and trustworthy work as a scientist has been honorably recognized in various ways. In 1876 he arranged the state collection of minerals at Albany. In 1882 he was appointed chemist to the New York State Board of Health, and performed valuable service in the analysis of articles of food. In 1884 he was called as an expert witness in the Jennie McGraw-Fiske will case, to value the collections of Cornell University.

In February, 1889, he was appointed by the Assembly of the State of New York, one of four experts to examine the new ceiling of the Assembly Chamber of the Capitol at Albany.

As a mining engineer, Professor Chester has made many explorations in distant localities, often in pathless solitudes, where questions of the highest importance were to be decided. In 1875 and 1880 he was engaged in exploring the great iron deposits of the Vermillion district in Minnesota. An account of this work is given in the "Eleventh Annual Report of the Geological Survey of Minnesota." Other explorations have been made in Ontario and Nova Scotia, in Michigan, Colorado, Nevada, California, Utah, Arkansas and Missouri. The investment of millions of dollars has been determined by Professor Chester's reports, and in no instance have his conclusions been found inaccurate or misleading.

Besides frequent contributions to scientific periodicals, Professor Chester is the author of "A Catalogue of Minerals, Alphabetically Arranged, with their Chemical Composition and Synonyms." This book was published in 1886, by John Wiley & Sons, New York. His preparation for this work was made with great thoroughness, and Dr. James A. H. Murray of Oxford, England, in the preface to the first volume of his "New English Dictionary on Historical Principles," makes acknowledgment of his obligations to Professor Chester for valuable aid in the history of mineralogical terms. His private library is enriched with many rare old books in his favorite departments of research.

In 1878 Professor Chester received, on examination, the degree of Doctor of Philosophy, from the trustees of Columbia College, an academic title amply earned by his pre-eminent success as a college instructor, by his unwearied devotion to scientific and scholarly pursuits, and his widely-known achievements as a mining engineer.

COLLEGE TRUSTEES.

More than one hundred and fifty honored men have rendered Hamilton College service as Trustees, since the Institution was chartered. On the long roll are names prominent in Church and State. Some of these eminent men gave the College almost a life service. The late General John Jay Knox, a merchant and banker may be instanced. He was a trustee for nearly fifty years. The love of a cultured family for Hamilton is illustrated in him and his. Four of his sons and four of his grandsons graduated there. The Rev. Dr. Wm. E. Knox, who was a trustee from 1876 until the year of his death, graduated in 1840. Hon. John Jay Knox, Ex-Comptroller of the National Currency, President of the National Bank of the Republic New York City, and a member of the

present Board of Trustees of the College, was in the class of 1849.
Hon. Henry M. Knox, a banker, graduated in 1851, and Rev. Dr.
Chas. E. Knox, President of the German Theological Seminary,
Newark, N. J., was in the class of 1856.

The chairman of the present Board, Hon. Henry A. Foster,
LL. D., has served fifty-three years. The late Samuel B. Wool-
worth, LL. D. served forty-four years. The late Dr. Simeon
North, forty-five years. and the late Hon. Horatio Seymour forty-
two years. A large number were trustees more than ten years.
The present Secretary of the Board of Trustees is the Rev. Dr.
Thos. B. Hudson.

The members of the present Board of Trustees are: Hon.
Henry A. Foster. LL. D., Rome, elected 1836: Hon. William J.
Bacon, LL. D., Utica, 1856; William D. Walcott, Esq., New
York Mills, 1863; Charles C. Kingsley, A. M., Utica, 1867; Rev.
L. Merrill Miller, D. D., Ogdensburg, 1869: Publius V. Rogers,
A. M., Utica, 1869; Gen. Samuel S. Ellsworth, A. M., Penn Yan,
1870: Rev. Henry Kendall, D. D., New York, 1871; Gilbert
Mollison, Esq., Oswego, 1871: Hon. Ellis H. Roberts, LL. D.,
Utica, 1872; Hon. Daniel P. Wood. A. M., Syracuse, 1874; Hon.
George M. Diven, A. M., Elmira, 1874: Hon. Theodore W.
Dwight, LL. D., New York, 1875; Hon. Joseph R. Hawley, LL. D.,
Hartford, Conn., 1875; Pres. David H. Cochran, Ph. D., LL. D.,
Brooklyn, 1875; Rev. James B. Lee, D. D., Franklinville, 1877;
Rev. James B. Shaw. D. D., Rochester, 1877: Pres. Henry Darl-
ing, D. D., LL. D., Clinton, 1880: Prof. Edward North, L. H. D.,
LL. D., Clinton, 1881; Hon. Elihu Root, A. M., New York, 1883;
Hon. John Jay Knox, A. M., New York, 1884; Charles A. Hawley
A. M., Seneca Falls, 1884; Rev. Thomas B. Hudson, D. D.,
Clinton, 1884: Horace B. Silliman, A. M., Cohoes, 1885; A.
Norton Brockway, A. M., M. D., New York, 1885; Rev. T.
Ralston Smith, D. D., Buffalo, 1886; Rev. George B. Spalding,
D. D., Syracuse, 1886; Hon. Theodore M. Pomeroy, A. M.,
Auburn, 1886: Rev. Thomas B. Hudson, D. D., *Secretary*, (1885),
and Treasurer, 1886; Charles A Borst, A. M., *Assistant to the
Treasurer*, 1881.

COLLEGE TREASURERS.

Seven Treasurers since 1812, have had the custody of the College
funds: Erastus Clark. (Dartmouth,) an able lawyer, James Dean,

(Union,) also a lawyer and fine classical scholar, Othniel Williams. (Yale,) another honored member of the bar, and a faithful college officer, Benjamin Woolsey Dwight, M. D., (Yale,) a ripe scholar and an accurate and methodical business man, Othniel Samuel Williams, LL. D., (Hamilton,) a man with a genius for business, and also a scholar of fine literary tastes, Publius V. Rogers, (Hamilton,) and the Rev. Thomas B. Hudson, D. D. (Hamilton,) for a time tutor in the College, and since 1870 Pastor of the Presbyterian Church in Clinton.

BEQUESTS AND SCHOLARSHIPS.

The first bequest received by Hamilton College was in 1832, when Hon. William H. Maynard, a member of the State Senate, died of Asiatic cholera in New York City, and left an endowment of twenty thousand dollars for the Chair of Law, History and Political Economy. An addition of ten thousand dollars to this fund was afterwards made by Hon. James Knox, of Knoxville, Illinois, who had been a law-student in the office of Senator Maynard. An endowment of thirty thousand dollars for the President's Chair was given by the late Benjamin S. Walcott and his son, William D. Walcott, of New York Mills, whose name is a synonym throughout Central New York, for integrity and Christian generosity. The endowment of thirty thousand dollars for the Observatory was given by the late Edwin C. Litchfield, of Brooklyn, a graduate of the College in 1832. The Professorship of Chemistry was endowed by the late Silas D. Childs, of Utica, and his wife Mrs. Roxana Childs, bequeathed sixty thousand dollars more. The Chair of Natural History was endowed by the late Mrs. Valeria Stone, of Malden, Massachusetts, and the Chair of Mathematics by the late Samuel Fletcher Pratt, of Buffalo. Honorable Gerrit Smith gave twenty thousand dollars for current expenses.

Many smaller bequests, permanent scholarships and timely gifts tell how the passing needs of a College will be provided for, when it faithfully performs its work in preparing young men for the highest duties in Church and State. An example of Christian beneficence has the power of an endless life. The good that good men do can never be buried with their bones. It multiplies itself in endless inspirations of good.

THE CURRICULUM.

The Hamilton Catalogue publishes as the aim of the College, the training of the mind to habits of accurate discrimination, close reasoning and vigorous application, and at the same time furnishing it with the leading facts and principles of Literature, Science and the Arts. To this end, while giving other branches due prominence, the study of Greek, Latin and Mathematics is required as furnishing the long-tested and approved means of mental discipline, invaluable to those who desire to lay a solid foundation for subsequent professional studies. The difference between a College and a University has been set forth in this sentence : " In a College you learn something about everything ; in a University, everything about something." The College aims to lay the broad foundation : the professional school concentrates the student's thoughts upon that which pertains to his proposed pursuit. The Hamilton curriculum is designed to be broad, but not superficial. Students are urged to read all they can on the subjects they are investigating. What Thomas Carlyle counseled a body of European students, they are counseled : " Count a thing known only after you have bounded it on the north, and bounded it on the south, and bounded it on the east and bounded it on the west."

A contributor to the columns of the " Hamilton Literary Monthly," having compared the Hamilton curriculum with that of an excellent New England College, (Williams,) writes :

" In the first place the requirements for admission are as nearly like our own as possible without their being exactly the same. Turning to their curriculum, we are unable to draw a strict comparison with our own, for they do not designate the amount of time given to the different subjects. For Freshman year the work is practically the same as our own. They have a provision for lectures on health and habits of study which we have not, while we provide for exercises in English Composition, and our courses in Greek and Latin are more comprehensive. They give no electives for Sophomore year and take up Natural History and Chemistry during spring term of that year. Mathematics as a required study ends with the second term as it does here. As regards Latin and Greek, they have one more term in Latin, for which we substitute French. German is required the first and second term

in a study of the grammar, prose reading and composition, taking
Schiller the last term. During Junior year the modern languages
are kept among the requirements, which is perhaps the most rad-
ical difference, (so far as one could judge,) between the *curric la*.
Their system of electives for upper-classmen years is not particularly intelligible to one not conversant with their methods. Latin
and Greek extend into Senior year as they do here now under the
regime adopted during this term. Leaving the electives, which
are in no way superior to our own, we find Physics and Astronomy
among the requirements for Junior year, which, with one term of
Political Economy, the modern languages as above noted, and
Rhetorical exercises similar to our own, constitute all their
required work for that year. We have Biblical study, Chemistry,
Law, and Theism as required studies instead of the languages.
The fall term of Senior year is precisely the same as our own in
the required studies, omitting two hours per week which we
devote to the study of Constitutional Law. In the other two
terms of Senior year there is little difference. We have one or
two branches put down as elective which they require, and *vice
versa*. Our catalogue all through is more precise
and explicit, and the information is just as abundant."

Hamilton, in the interests of scholarship, seeks
to reach young men, even before they enter its
precincts, by offering a prize from the fund founded
by Dr. A. Norton Brockway, of New York, to the
student who passes the best examination in preparatory studies. All through the course, scholarship
is rewarded with gold and silver medals and money prizes. College honors and Φ. B. K. keys await the young graduates who have
maintained high standing during undergraduate years. More than
thirty prizes are offered those who excel in Greek, Latin, Mathematics, German, French, Natural Philosophy, Mental Philosophy,
Biblical Science, English Composition, and Original Oratory.
Recently Chauncey S. Truax, Esq., of New York City, established a fund, the interest of which will be awarded to that
member of the Senior class, who maintains the highest rank
in Greek studies of the first three years of the undergraduate
course. The income of this scholarship is two hundred dollars.
A similar fund has been established for the mathematical

department. Twenty-four scholarships have been established, which vary in their annual income from sixty to one hundred dollars. Enthusiasm for thorough work, which characterizes young men of studious habit, directed by these various prizes and honors, must result in scholarship. One of the younger alumni of Hamilton, Dr. A. C. White, now a Professor at Cornell, has recently written a volume in Latin, which has received merited honor.

The classical scholarship of another Hamiltonian has been recognized in the appointment of Dr. Isaac H. Hall, one of the curators of the Metropolitan Museum of Art in New York City. The published proceedings of the American Oriental Society contain many learned and valuable papers by Dr. Hall who graduated at Hamilton in 1859. He was the first scholar in America, who mastered the peculiar Greek dialect of the Cypriote inscriptions, as he found them on the Cypriote antiquities discovered by General di Cesnola on the sites of ancient Idalium and Golgos. That Dr. Hall should have made this very important discovery, while a young New York lawyer, who could give to this study only his broken hours of leisure, reflects special credit on the College where he received his classical training.

BELLES-LETTRES AND ORATORY.

The reputation of Hamilton College has been greatly widened by her strenuous advocacy of the study of belles-lettres and oratory. The aim is to teach students how to record and voice thought, to graduate young men who will write with musical pens, and speak, not in sleepy monotones, but with natural and effective accents, "ringing all the bells in the chime," commanding and rewarding attention. The Rev. Dr. John Wayland, brother of Ex-President Wayland, of Brown University, the Rev. Dr. Henry Mandeville, the Rev. Dr. James R. Boyd, the Rev. Dr. Anson Judd Upson, the Rev. Samuel D. Wilcox, A. M., the Rev. Dr. Henry A. Frink, the Rev. Arthur S. Hoyt, A. M., and Prof. Clinton Scollard, A. M., have served the College in the department of logic, rhetoric and elocution. The last two are still in the College Faculty.

At the Intercollegiate Convention in the Academy of Music, New York, both years when Hamilton students competed, they carried off the prizes for elocution, although their cultured contestants were students from such colleges as Princeton, Lafayette, Williams,

Cornell, Rutgers, University of New York, Syracuse University, North Western University and St. John's College. In honor of the prizes won by Hamilton students in this competition, three Binghamton gentlemen presented the Professor of Rhetoric fifteen hundred dollars for the purchase of recent books in polite literature. These volumes constitute a part of the Rhetorical library to which recent additions have been made in annotated editions of English classics for the especial use of classes in English literature.

THE MAYNARD-KNOX LAW SCHOOL.

The Maynard-Knox Law School has added to the roll of Hamiltonians two hundred and fifty-three names. Theodore W. Dwight, LL. D., a graduate of Hamilton, and now the distinguished Warden of Columbia College Law School, New York City, Ellicott Evans, LL. D., an alumnus of Harvard, and Francis M. Burdick, A. M., a graduate of Hamilton and now Professor of Jurisprudence in Cornell University, have been professors in this law school. Hon. Wm. Curtis Noyes, LL. D., an honorary alumnus of Hamilton, after a life of eminent service, professional and political, bequeathed the College his law library. The collection numbers about five thousand volumes. The books were collected during a practice of over twenty-five years, at a cost of not less than sixty thousand dollars.

THE CAMPUS.

Not many parks in the land afford more beautiful views than Hamilton College Campus, with its winding foot-paths, carriage drives, shade trees, shrubbery, hedges, and class stones. A long row of tall poplars, like old continentals in line, sentinel the classic halls. The trees were brought from Philadelphia, whither they had been imported by Thomas Jefferson from Lombardy. They were planted on College Hill between 1804-8 under the direction of Samuel Kirkland and his daughter. The beauties of the Campus are supplemented by Professor Root's garden, where sylvan shades, fragrant flowers and the "liquid lip" of a babbling brook invite the student who loves nature. Scattered through the Campus are class trees, planted by graduating classes, and marked by memorial marbles and granites, hewn and unhewn, and of various designs. These monuments are inscribed with class mottoes, such as

Ἔργα πρὸ λόγων. Ἀλήθεια καὶ νίκη. Ἡμῖν Ἴλλον Ἀθήνης. Κράτος κρατοῦσι. Μηδαμῶς ἔχνια ἀζ᾽. Σοφία τὸ πρώτιστον. Οὐκ ἐθάνομεν ἔτι. Ἔκαστος πᾶσι, πάντες ἑκάστῳ. Τέλος ἀρετή κρατεῖ. Τόλμησον, μὴ δ'ἄγαν τόλμησον.

THE COLLEGE HALLS.

Upwards of thirty buildings in Clinton roof the Faculty and Students, the class-rooms, libraries, fraternities, cabinets and apparatus of the College. South College is a "store house of memories." A few years ago, through the generosity of Hon. John H. Hungerford, "Old South" was remodelled and improved. It is now known as Hungerford Hall. Middle College is called Kirkland Hall. North College, formerly known as Dexter Hall, having been repaired and improved, is called after the name of the generous gentleman who enabled the Trustees to make these changes—Wm. H. Skinner Hall.

In the observatory, in addition to the large telescope, which is mounted on a granite shaft, are a portable Transit instrument, an astronomical clock, a chronograph, a siderial chronometer, an aneroid barometer and two fine portable telescopes. The building has been connected by a telegraphic wire with the nearest station, and the longitude of the observatory has thus been accurately determined by exchanging star signals with the Harvard College Observatory at Cambridge, Mass. In its turn the observatory on College Hill has become the basis of several longitudes in the State and of the longitude of Detroit Observatory at Ann Arbor, Michigan, which latter forms the fundamental point for the longitude of the lake survey. The latest work of this kind has been to determine the longitude of the western boundary of the State of New York. The zone star observations taken at Litchfield Observatory, now number over 100,000. Twenty of the celestial charts, for which the zone stars form the skeleton, were published four years ago, (at private expense), and distributed gratuitously from the Litchfield Observatory to other observatories, learned societies and private individuals, in return for favors received. The late Edwin C. Litchfield, LL. D., of Brooklyn, liberally endowed the chair of astronomy and the observatory which is named in his honor.

The Perry H. Smith Library Hall furnishes space for sixty thousand volumes. In this building are the Edward Robinson, the Wm. Curtis Noyes, the Truax, and the Mears libraries. An interesting apartment in the library building is the Memorial Hall and Art Gallery. It is set aside for "historical paintings, landscapes, plaster casts, figures in bronze and marble, engravings, tablets, ancient coins and other works of art, along with autographs and portraits of distinguished alumni and of officers and benefactors of the College." Here are portraits of the Rev. Samuel Kirkland, the Rev. Samson Occum, the Indian Orator, Presidents Backus, Davis, North, and Fisher, Dr. Edward Robinson, Professors Catlin, Avery and North, Hon. Gerrit Smith, the Rev. Albert Barnes, Hon. Henry A. Foster, Judge Charles H. Truax, Hon. John Jay Knox, Wm. C. Noyes, Silas D. Childs and others prominent in church or state or college. Here is also a portrait bust of the Hon. Edwin C. Litchfield, by Hiram Powers. Among portrait painters represented are Huntington, Spencer, Elliott, Andrews, Wells, Healy, Peebles and Carpenter. The first named of these artists, Daniel Huntington, President of the National Academy of Design, was at one time a student at Hamilton. While in College he painted upon "bass-wood canvas," a portrait of the College janitor, "Professor Twitchell," who "one day as he was going his dusty rounds was quite willing to rest awhile in the young artist's room and be "booked for immortality." This portrait is still preserved in the College library with a label in the Greek professor's "eagle-quill chirography:" "*Τα μέλλοντα προσκιαζει.*" "coming events cast their shadows before." Here are also portraits of students who fell in battle for their country.

The late Hon. James Knox, LL.D., of Knoxville, Ill., bequeathed a fund to the College, which has enabled the trustees to complete the Knox Hall of Natural History. Students interested in plants find the Sartwell Herbarium of great value, and the Barlow collections afford fine facilities for those especially interested in ornithology and entomology. In the Laboratory is suitable apparatus for the use of students of chemistry. Those who wish to become more thoroughly acquainted with mineralogy find the extensive College collections of great service.

Old alumni of Hamilton College will be surprised as they wander up the "old poplar" walk to South College, to see a handsome brick building of modified Romanesque style, confronting them at the entrance to the campus, near South College, says the Utica *Herald*. It stands like a porter's lodge, guarding the gate, and the fitness of such a guardian will be recognized when it is known that it is to be the home of the Young Men's Christian Association of the College. The building was erected through the generosity of Horace B. Silliman, of Cohoes, who is one of the Trustees of the College, and equally interested in Education and Christian Association work. Mr. Silliman was a prominent member of the late State Convention of the Y. M. C. A., held at Watertown. His connection with the College Association at Old Hamilton will be more than simply providing a comfortable and even luxurious home for it, but will take the form of personal interest in its welfare. Yet it is but proper to add, that to the Christian young men of the College belongs some of the credit of this elegantly appointed Hall, for had they not labored faithfully in Christian work and for their fellow students, the donor would not have felt like bestowing such a valuable piece of property upon the institution. The Association at Hamilton College stands higher in interest and results than any other Association, and this building will not detract from its usefulness or zeal. The structure is of Deerfield red brick, with heavy brown stone trimmings. A tower at the southeast end terminates in a covered balcony or observatory. The tower is about the same height as the peak of the main roof, and is very graceful, giving a finish to the eastern facade. The facade contains, on the right, the main entrance, under a protected arch or vestibule of brown stone, over which are several Roman windows, and a recessed balcony built in the wall. The gables are neatly capped and trimmed, and are at right angles.

On the right of the vestibule is the reading room, 18x30 feet, well lighted and finished in oak, with open fire-place, and door leading to pleasant parlor in the rear. On the left is a handsome refreshment room, 19x20 feet. Near the entrance are the cloak room and Secretary's office. The cellar contains ample storage room, and a Cohoes steam heater, with a patent steam register under the hall. A curved stairway and balustrade lead to the second floor. There a pleasant suite of rooms is found, part of which are for the Association President, or Secretary. A large room for prayer meetings and similar gatherings occupies the main portion of this floor, being separable into two rooms by folding doors. There is also a small committee-room. The rooms are all handsomely ceiled and finished, and well heated

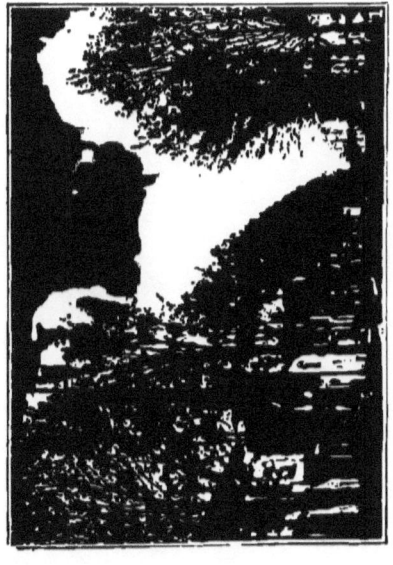

and ventilated. The wood work is in the natural oak. A narrow stairway leads to the half story above, where there are a commodious loft and two "summer rooms" opening out into a balcony, the wooden floor of which is laid over a tin roofing. From these, there is a fine view of the college grounds. In the basement of the buildings are to be baths, supplied with hot and cold water. The college boys may well thank Mr. Silliman for his generous gift, which, when complete, will have cost him over $20,000.

The thoughtful spectator looking out from the balcony of the Y. M. C. A. Hall, will rapidly survey a century's changes and improvements* on College Hill. Before him will appear a multitude of thoughtful faces, youthful and old, and the forms of many men, Indian and whites. He will see Kirkland and Schenandoa and Steuben laying the corner-stone of the first building. He will see the Principals and Students of the old Oneida Academy going in and out. Then will follow a long procession, in which he will see many eminent and godly men—College Trustees, Benefactors, Presidents, Professors and Students. The dates of the erection of the various buildings testify to the uninterrupted efforts of the friends of learning, and of Christianity to enrich the minds and purify the hearts of successive student generations.

---

* Hamilton Oneida Academy, corner-stone laid 1793. Commons Hall, built 1813, used as Mineralogical Cabinet 1850, remodeled as Knox Hall of Natural History 1883. South College (Hamilton Hall), erected 1814, remodeled and renamed, (Hungerford Hall, 1871. Middle College, (Oneida Hall, erected 1797). Kirkland Hall erected 1822. North College, walls built 1824, completed as Dexter Hall 1842, remodeled and renamed, (Wm. H. Skinner Hall). 1881. Chapel erected 1825-7, refurnished by the Hon. Truman P. Handy, Cleveland, Ohio, 1882. College Bell presented by Mr. Daniel Nolton, Holland Patent, N. Y. Motto on Bell, *Ora et Labora*, (Pray and Labor); Clock in Chapel spire, presented by the Hon. John Wanamaker, Philadelphia, Penna., 1877. Hamilton Oneida Academy pulled down 1829. Gymnasium erected 1853. Litchfield Observatory erected 1854; Telescope Mounted, 1857, Observatory enlarged, 1875, Chemical Laboratory erected 1855. Perry H. Smith Library Hall, corner-stone laid 1870, completed 1872. Silliman Hall, (Y. M. C. A. Building), erected 1888. Society Halls — go to Phi Place, corner-stone laid 1871, completed 1873. Alpha Delta Phi Lodge, (Eels Memorial), corner-stone laid 1876, completed 1883. Chi Psi House, purchased 1882, remodeled 1884. Psi Upsilon House, erected 1885. Delta Kappa Epsilon House, purchased 1882, burned Aug. 17, 1886, rebuilt 1888. Delta Upsilon House, erected 1888. Theta Delta Chi House, etc. built 1888. In 1853, the campus park was laid out at a cost of $800. At that time the stone walls, etc., were removed to make room for hedges. Previous to this date a continued walk extended in front of the Halls as now, and paths from North College, South College and the Chapel lead to the openings in the fence in front. The original College campus was a rectangular plot of four acres. The plan of those having charge of improvements was to bring under cultivation about twenty acres of land immediately surrounding the college buildings. This would include the plot especially designated for an ornamental use by Mr. Kirkland in his deed to the Trustees of the Hamilton Oneida Academy.

NATURE'S GYMNASIUM.

The old institution at Clinton possesses one advantage the value of which is inestimable. Its location is as healthful as it is charming. Physical vigor is indispensible to the brainworker. "Health is the bed-plate of the mental machinery." A scholar without health is a shorn Samson. College Hill is nature's gymnasium. The College and the Hill co-operate, the one to bestow all the refinement of an Attic culture, with which to crown the vigor of the Spartan discipline the other furnishes. A student writes: "The College is about four thousand feet above the level of the sea and still rising. The climate is peculiar. The zephyrs which steal so gently over the land, knocking down trees, throwing cars off the track and destroying villages, come from here. They all start back of the College barn, and never go the other way." The Rev. Dr. Andrew Hull, Class of '36, in the Half-Century Letter, read three years ago, says: "I very gratefully remember the arduous walks down and up College Hill, with a cane across my back, holding the elbows in line as I walked and inhaled through the nostrils, and puffed full volumes of breath explosively from the mouth. In due time my somewhat deformed chest was so expanded that the ribs formed a perfect arch, and the lungs had ample room for their essential work. Possibly the now popular athletic sports would have done the same thing for me; but the exercise I took in the way described was sufficient, without the supplements of bruises, sprains, and ponderous hands."

COLLEGE PUBLICATIONS.

The annual and triennial catalogues of the Institution, supplemented by three publications edited by the undergraduates, keep the alumni informed as to the events in the College world. The "Hamilton Literary Monthly," conducted by the Senior Class, is in the twenty-fourth volume. It holds a high place among college periodicals. "The Dartmouth Lit." recently said, "To be copied by the Lit. of Yale, or Williams, or Harvard or Hamilton, or by other truly excellent college journals, places the seal of an appreciation outside of one's own country, and incites the writer to better efforts." "The Hamilton Review" is published by the Emersonian society, and "The Hamiltonian" by the Fraternity men of the

Junior Class. "The Hamiltonian" is a mirror of college life. It knows its place. Its own language is:

"Loyalty is a sentiment, and it is of the heart first. There must be more than mere feeling. For, while loyal hearts cling long and faithfully, as in the devotion of the Scotch and English Jacobites to the Stuarts; yet in the end, lack of respect will stifle even loyalty. So we are glad of thorough work, honest dealing and no humbug in College. But these alone will not awake earnest loyalty.

"The heart which beats loyally throbs by instants, and it is the little things, the things oft hidden, of daily life, that link the heart-throbs to any object—to home, to oft frequented haunts, to school, to college, and make one loyal to it.

"Those who, from year to year, come back to Hamilton, and at anniversary feasts recall their college days, are wont to talk, not of ablative absolute, optative moods, functions of X, precipitate, Roman law and such like; but of what "the boys" did in their far college days, and how they looked at life, and how life seemed to them. While the locks have whitened and the strength abated, while the thought has widened and the judgment mightily matured—the hearts that were here in the 30s, the 40s, the 50s, and the 60s, come back and are warm as they were then. So the inner things of college life are worth talking of, worth remembering. To embalm some of these in print "The Hamiltonian" exists. It means more and other than the catalogue: that speaks to brains and judgment for the work-side of college: we speak to hearts and to feelings, for the home-side, the play-side, the heart-side of college life."

STUDENT ANNALS.

Ah! yes, what "the boys" did would furnish material for a volume, which might not always sustain the dignity of history, but would be perused with keen delight by hundreds of widely-scattered graduates in their counting rooms, libraries and offices, recalling those Sophomoric days when neither the weight of years nor of dignity oppressed them—those days when a meeting of Parliament or Senate did not concern them so much as a Faculty meeting, and the startling summons of "Pete," "Ho! Brown, stick your head out. Faculty wants you; pack your trunk!"

When Professor J. R. Green, of Oxford University, England,

sat down to write a history of his country, he determined not to
make it a record of English Kings and conquests, "a drum and
trumpet history," but a history of the English *people*. The Hamilton historian, who will write the annals, not of the administra-
tions of College Presidents, but of student life, will have many
alumni readers. He will not fail to record those conversations in
the far-off days, when the century was young, and when men now
gray-haired and eminent, sat as happy students around open fire-
places cracking jokes as thoroughly seasoned as the dry back-logs
which the laughing flames cracked. He will picture the frosty
six-o'clock chapel, as seen by tallow-candle light, and the old village church, with its "fire of devotion and foot stoves," and good
Dr. Norton preaching in cloak and mittens.

"PROF." PETER BLAKE.

Among the illustrations, he
might include the College din-
ing hall, "the Commons," with
the "buttery" underneath, well-
supplied with strong beer, cider,
chewing tobacco and cigars, the
profits of the sales of which,
were the perquisites of some
worthy charity student. That
was before the days of the
blessed Temperance Reforma-
tion. Knowing that a more
grave history has put on record
the public services of, for instance, such a philanthropist
as Gerrit Smith, our historian
would not depict him as he
appeared in the Halls of Congress, a conspicuous statesman, but as
he appeared to the College President, with his conspicuous boots
protruding from under the bed, whither he had beat a precipitous
retreat, and from which scholastic cloister he promptly replied to
the question, "Gerrit, what are you doing there?" "Meditating,
sir!" To the pages of our student history the reader would not
refer to find the public discourses of the eloquent Dr. Joel Parker,
but there he would find the report of his discourse with a tutor, who
after the term opening, was calling late arrivals to a strict account.
"Parker," said he. Parker arose to his feet. "Sir." "Parker, you

FROM LOCKWOOD'S FRATERNITY STATIONERY,
BY PERMISSION OF LOCKWOOD & COOMBES, 275 FIFTH AVENUE, N. Y.

BADGES WORN BY HAMILTON COLLEGE FRATERNITY MEN

did not appear until Friday." "No, sir; I did not." "Did you
bring a written excuse from your parents?" "I have no parents,"
was the laconic reply. "Did you bring an excuse from your
guardian?" "I have no guardian." "From your friends?" "I
have no friends." The tutor ceased; the class laughed; and Joel
Parker's classmates thereafter never ceased to characterize him as
the man, who had neither friends nor relatives.

Upon the pages of our student annals might not be found such
words as President, Peters, North, Oren Root, Sr., and Oren Root,
Jr., but the Hamiltonian would understand their substitutes,
"Prex," "Twinkle," "Greek," "Cube Root," "Square Root."
No chapter would be devoted to Geometry or Calculus, but space
would be reserved for the erudite definition which a precocious
student of mathematics, who afterward was prominent in the nation,
gave in response to the question: "Mr. E. what is a curved line?"
"A curved line is a straight line on a bender, sir!" A copy of a
certain college diploma, might not be in the annals, but the annal-
ist would account for its absence in the very words of the student
who did not remain to graduate: "Hamilton college has turned
out a good many good men, it turned me out!" Not with alge-
braic signs would these student annals be sprinkled over, but they
would abound with significant words and sentences, recalling
class meetings, college politics, the army of the Oriskany, "ringing off the rust," "fresh!" Sophomore arbor; "road!" Chum,
snatches of class songs, serenades, chapel exercises, recitation
halls, the College color, the "bear box," bonfires, foot ball, base
ball, "the elopement of a bell, whose gender was neuter," fraternity life, burial of books, class rides, tree planting, class poems and
prophecies, and hosts of pursuits not included in the curriculum as
required studies, but "elected" successively by grandsire, sire and
grandson as indispensable to a liberal education.

The stars which the renowned and patient Peters has discovered
might not be catalogued in our student volume, but every Hamiltonian would value the book if it could reproduce for him those
sweetly beaming stars of his student life as he dreamed of them,
while looking across the moon-lit Oriskany to the opposite hillside
where fair, bright-eyed maidens graced seminary halls. How they
are remembered let a recent response to a toast by Mr. A. M.
Griswold, editor of the *Texas Siftings*, at the reunion of a Greek
Letter Fraternity testify.

"The Girls We Left Behind Us."

"Mr. President and Brothers: The toast you have assigned me is one that touches a very tender chord in my heart. I have always felt sorry for the girls we left behind us. It seemed cruel at the time, but how could we help it? Circumstances were such that we couldn't take them along; we had to leave them behind us. I think I promised three or four to come back for them in the spring or early autumn, but I was too busy for several years to attend to it, and after that—well, I was afraid my wife might not like it. I met one of the girls we left behind us in the street to-day. That is, I thought I did. The same soft, brown eyes, the same sweet, sunny smile.

'Is it possible,' I said, that 'I behold Miss Sally Jones!'

'That was my mother's name,' she smiled, 'before she was married. I am married now, and I have named my baby after ma.'

Great heavens! The girl I left behind me is a grandmother!

I told the young lady who I was, and she said she had often heard her mother speak of me as one she used to know a great many years ago. Then I asked about the girls I used to know, and what had become of them. I found that some, alas, are dead. Others, who were married, wished they were dead. Some, who were widows, had lovers seeking for their hands. Others, not yet widows, were seeking for divorces.

Oh, those seminary girls of long ago—how we did regret leaving them behind us—except one poor fellow who eloped with one of them. He has regretted all his life that he didn't leave her behind with the rest of them.

But we had to go and leave them. Fate beckoned us on. And, in some cases, the faculty urged us to go. Were we to blame, then, for temporarily forgetting the debts—I mean the girls we left behind us? Why, some of us had to leave our trunks!

A rare collection of girls they were, gentlemen, as I recall them now. Tall, willowy girls; short, plump girls; black-eyed girls that made us blue, and blue-eyed girls that we were ready to take a black eye for any time; fair-complexioned girls, Brown girls, Smith girls, girls with auburn hair, and girls who, not being able to match their own hair in Auburn, were compelled to buy it in

Beneath the Poplar tree."

RETROSPECTIVE. [SEE PAGE 85.]

Utica or Syracuse. In fact there was about every kind of girl then that there is now, except the tailor-made girl, who seems to be altogether a modern creation. Still, the latter has points in her favor. While the girl I so tenderly recall possessed virtue, beauty, intelligence and many engaging ways, I must admit that she somehow lacked the get-up of the girl of to-day."

After reading the volume at whose contents we have hinted, the oldest graduate would feel his pulse beating faster, perhaps his eyes moistening, and though his age-cracked voice or his dignity might prevent his giving the college yeil, "Rah! Rah!! Rah!!! Hamil-ton! Zip-rah-boom!" he would be ready to join in the chorus of Professor North's

RETROSPECTIVE.

" Alumni! now I'm going to sing
  A song that home will come;
Of happy moments that I've known
  With my old College chum.
How I wish that I could roam again
  Beside the Oriskany,
Or with my chum could sit and talk
  Beneath the Poplar tree.

    CHORUS—'Tis many a night since first we sat
        Beneath the Poplar tree,
        And there made glad the hours with fun,
        And laugh, and minstrelsy

" Four years went by on pinions light,
  And then the distant hum
Of dull toil, bade me leave my books
  And my old College chum.
But I dream by night when all is still,
  That he comes back to me,
And golden hours return again
  Beneath the Poplar tree.

    CHORUS.

' I might forget that I have reached
  The half of years four-score,
When I can dream I see my chum
  And hail him Sophomore.
Would Alma Mater's grandsons cease
  To climb their father's knee,
And tease me funny tales to tell
  About the Poplar tree.

    CHORUS.

THE END.

www.ingramcontent.com/pod-product-compliance
Lightning Source LLC
Chambersburg PA
CBHW032014010726
47493CB00007B/2401